Soulmate

Soulmate

Jason Owen

To order additional copies of this book, contact:
Xlibris Corporation
1-888-795-4274
www.Xlibris.com
Orders@Xlibris.com
94668

CONTENTS

ACKNOWLEDGEMENTS

I would like to thank God, for without His continued help, I would never have even gotten the idea for the story.

I thank all of my family and church family for their support; I could not have done this without your encouraging words.

To my friends, there are so many of you I am afraid to name because I am sure I would leave someone out and I never wish to do that but I do have to say a special thank you to Marcus Mayweather and Ana Alicia Perez for them allowing me to name the two wolf pups after them.

A special thank you to Dick Petrie for allowing me to use his photograph of the two wolves, I knew I was in God's will when I saw that photograph because that picture was the one I saw in my head before I saw it on your website. It was God who led me to it.

Dr. William Hearth stared out the window of the hospital room at the gloomy clouds that had started to gather in the sky outside. He watched as they slowly choked the sun and forced its rays to fade until there was nothing but the darkness of rain in the atmosphere. The ominous sky with its raven clouds cast a dim shadow over the professor's light blue eyes.

"It will rain soon." He whispered to himself.

"Dr. Hearth, it is time." Dr. Rosen, his wife's Oncologist, said in a gentle manner.

Dr. Hearth moved from the window slowly. As dreary as the scene was outside, it still was not as dark as the one in that hospital room but he was not about to let on how he felt to anyone. Ever since his wife Rose had been diagnosed with cancer, he had descended slowly into a strict cold analytical demeanor. He had always been that way at his job but when his wife was near, he came alive with passion and even sometimes was as giddy as a teenager in love because that was the relationship they had for all the years of their courtship and marriage.

However the events that of the past year had eroded his passion and brought out the scientist in him all of the time. The year had begun so hopeful because they reached a comfortable level in their respective occupations and they decided to have children. It was at her checkup that they received the news that would alter their lives and relationship. The doctor informed Rose that they had discovered a mass in her left breast and after the biopsy, confirmed that it was cancerous. But what was even more devastating, was that she had a rare form of aggressive carcinoma that was going to end her life in a few months. The doctor promised that she would be taken care of by

the best Oncologist in the state, which led them to Dr. Rosen's door.
He treated her cancer as combative as any one doctor could but the
disease had reached a dire point and had become incurable. William
had been there for his wife at every checkup and treatment but his
zeal for love and life had vanished. By the time Rose was in the final
stages and had to be put on a machine to keep her alive, William had
all of the arrangements for her funeral made. All he had to do was
wait for her to die.

He stood at the foot of his wife's bed and looked at her motionless
body. Dr. Rosen and Nurse Smyth had been there caring for her the
entire time since Rose Hearth had come to the hospital. Dr. Rosen
nodded to Nurse Smyth to prep Ms. Rose, as they had come to call
her, for taking her off life support. When all of the necessary measures
were completed, Nurse Smyth looked over at Dr. Rosen and gave him
a nod to tell him that he could complete the process. Dr. Rosen put his
hand on the machine to press the button to turn it off but he wanted
to make certain that Dr. Hearth understood what would take place.

"Dr. Hearth there maybe some residual echoes on the EKG
monitor but they will trail off soon. I want you to understand that
we do not believe that Rose will suffer anymore. Basically, she will
just go to sleep. You can move by her side if you like."

"I am fine here at the foot of the bed Dr. Rosen. Just do what you
have to do and I will do what I have to do, like I have been doing for
months now." He said coldly.

"Very well, sir." Dr. Rosen said as he swallowed the urge to
retort back to Dr. Hearth's curtness and turned back to look at the
monitor.

Dr. Rosen gave Nurse Smyth a quick glance as if to ask her with
his eyes if he had said something offensive and Nurse Smyth returned
a shocked look back at him that gave him some comfort that he had
been sensitive and that it was Dr. Hearth that was cold.

Dr. Rosen remembered when he had first met the couple at a
benefit for the zoo two years ago. He had not known them as patients
at that time, all he could think of was how hopeful and passionate

they were. He had enjoyed getting to know Dr. Hearth and Mrs. Rose and had learned that they were the talk of the town about how in love they were. They were the proverbial 'joined at the hip' couple. They had so much in common that they seemed to be the perfect match for each other. The only difference was their careers. Rose Hearth was an artist, not world renowned but famous in her region of the country. Dr. William Hearth was a Zoologist at the local Zoological Gardens who supervised the Wild Canine Exhibit. Her work was creative and his work was Scientific, two opposite ends of a wide spectrum or perhaps two ends of a circle that met with their union but Dr. Rosen knew all of that had changed now and let the thought pass out of his mind as they all waited for Rose to take her last breath.

These thoughts that had brought a small piece of joy and comfort to Dr. Rosen did not rattle about in Dr. Hearth's mind right now though. Three weeks ago, Rose had become unresponsive and ever since then William had gone into an even more rigid scientific frame of mind as a way of keeping the feelings of loss at bay while he pushed through this bog of dismal emotions. His plan had worked thus far and he was able to schedule all of the services and greet everyone who came, with the utmost of professional standards but everyone would all say, under their breath, that William was not himself. He was not a very emotional person, more analytical than anything else, except when he was with Rose. But with Rose's impending death, it seemed that he had lost something deep inside that they all hoped he would regain soon.

William stood at the foot of the bed and held a firm grip on his cold demeanor as Dr. Rosen moved to the machine again. William watched the monitor as it registered the frail heartbeats of his wife. He looked at her withered and still body as it lay helpless in the bed. Then, as he looked at her there, an emotional tsunami washed over him as he came to realize that the machine was about to stop her heart from beating. Time seemed to stand still for him as his mind forced him to turn and face the emotions he had suppressed.

Pictures flashed in his mind of a time when he had arranged an intimate picnic on the floor of the zoo's aquarium. The rainbow of colorful fish gracefully paraded by as they ate their sandwiches and held each other in a tight embrace. Then, William's mind took him back to the time when he proposed to her at a movie theater. As they waited for the movie to begin, a screen appeared with his proposal and as she stood in shock to read the screen. In front of everyone, he knelt down and presented her the ring. With her eyes filled with tears of joy, she accepted. Just as he was getting comfortable with the images, he was rushed to one last memory of the first time he met her. They were in an art class that William did not care for but needed the credit and as he struggled to grasp Cubism, she offered her help. She wore the same flowing white dress with lace trim that came down to her knees. The same one that she wore every time she worked, except at that time it was new. He would tell her later, that she looked like an angel when she sat down beside him. That day they became more than just classmates, stronger than friends and more passionate than lovers. They became something much more.

"STOP!" William yelled to Dr. Rosen and scared the poor Oncologist away from the life support machine. Nurse Smyth jumped aside too as William rushed to his wife's side. Family and friends, who had been outside of the room watching, at William's request, now hurried into the room to see what was the matter. No one said a word as they all watched as William weep uncontrollably as he held the lifeless body of his beloved in his arms.

William stroked her pink scarf covered head as he remembered what her beautiful blonde hair looked like before the breast cancer chemo ate it all away. He so wanted to get a look at her emerald eyes but they had been closed for a while now. He professed his love to her as if the two were alone in the room, and in his mind, they were. This was the outpouring of emotion he had tried so hard to avoid and now he felt that he had betrayed her love and was trying to make it up to her.

Dr. Rosen motioned with his hands for everyone to leave and give William a few more moments alone with his wife to say goodbye. Everyone had left the room but him, William and Rose. Dr. Rosen moved over to William and put his hand on the weeping man's shoulder.

"Dr. Hearth . . . . William, we are going to give you a little more time. I am just going to step . . . . "

"No, finish what you were doing." William interrupted with cracking voice as tears streamed down his face like a river.

Dr. Rosen nodded and moved back into position at the monitor.

"Dr. Rosen . . . . may I . . . . (William cleared his throat to gain some composure) . . . . May I hold her as you . . . . ?" William stammered through the tears and looked at the monitor as he spoke.

Dr. Rosen felt himself force back a tear as he understood what William was asking. He made certain that he kept up his level of composure as he responded.

"Of course William. Would you like to have your family and friends in here too?"

William nodded and Dr. Rosen motioned for them to enter as they all looked on through the glass at the scene in the room. They filed into the room and surrounded William and Rose as Dr. Rosen carefully turned off the life support machine. William held Rose tightly in his arms as he listened to the heart monitor beeps slowly start to decrease and fade into the deathly final sound of the flat line. Dr. Rosen quickly silenced the monitor to allow the horrid sound to end. William looked at Rose one last time and said the only thing that was in his heart.

"I Love You."

(AFTER THE FUNERAL
& AT THE ZOO)

Dr. Robert Nelson walked around the zoo greeting patrons and zoo professionals like he did every day. He was not like the other zoo professionals in the sense that they all had a background in the animal world. As the director of the zoo, his focus was more on business and bringing prestige to the zoo but his greatest quality was that he understood that none of his employees worked for him. They worked for the animals and the patrons that came to the zoo to feel a connection with nature which was the secret to the success of the zoo.

Dr. Bob, as he was affectionately known by his people, enjoyed seeing the workers and the patrons enjoying a sunny day at the zoo, until he came to the Canine Exhibit. Standing next to a column in the Wolf enclosure, he spied a very gloomy looking individual. He appeared to be just staring out into the area aimlessly. The man was wearing a suit but it appeared that he had been wearing the suit for quite some time and had not bothered to change. Dr. Bob reached into the inner jacket pocket of his coat and pulled out his walkie talkie.

"Security to the Wolf enclosure of the Canine exhibit please." He quietly called.

Dr. Bob wanted to keep an eye on the man until Security arrived but then, as he assessed the situation further, he noticed that the man was not really posing any sort of threat to the people or the animals. Dr. Bob got his courage up and decided to approach the man. As he neared him, Dr. Bob began to notice that the disheveled man looked familiar. Finally, he got within a few feet of the man and recognized him completely.

"Dr. Hearth? Are you all right?"

"I'm fine. I just wanted to see my kids." He said with a smile.

"Dr. Hearth, I was not aware you had any children? As a matter of fact, I remember hearing you yourself speak about how you and your wife should have tried for children sooner before she developed cancer?"

Dr. Bob then put together why Dr. Hearth was wearing a suit.

"Wait a moment! Today was your wife's funeral! Please tell me you were in attendance!"

"Of course I was! I was there and listened to everyone tell me about how sorry they were for my loss."

"Well, I believe after the funeral it is customary to go back to the deceased's home and fellowship more with the surviving family."

"I am aware of the custom, Dr. Bob." William said out of the corner of his mouth without taking his focus off 'His kids'.

"Then why are you here and not there?" He asked rather pointedly.

Dr. Hearth did not immediately respond to Dr. Bob's question. He just stared out at the two young wolves playing alone in the area. They both were from exactly the same litter but they appeared totally different. The male, named Marcus was a dark shade of sable and his sister, Ana, was a mixture of tans and whites, yet the two played together without any sort of anger, jealousy or problems of any kind, very unlike the best of any siblings. The one feature that did stick out about them was their 'birth marks'. There was a pattern in their furs that resembled a small heart. Dr. Hearth just sat there and marveled at the sight but Dr. Bob still wanted an answer to his question.

"Dr. Hearth, did you hear me? Why are you . . . ?"

"How many times have I asked you to call me William, Dr. Bob?" Dr. Hearth interrupted.

"Well, I suppose several but I am not used to greeting a professional with his first name."

"Indulge me please, just for today."

"Very well . . . . William. Why are you here and not at home?"

"I answered that question. I wanted to check on our kids." William said as he pointed out into the enclosure at the two wolf pups.

"You call them your . . . kids?" Dr. Bob asked raising his eyebrows as he spoke.

"Rose and I were going to try to have children in our third year of marriage which that was this year but this year proved to be full of an unwanted development. Instead of children, my wife had breast cancer. Well, about the time we found that out was when the two orphan wolves arrived here and I told her that we could name them and that they would be our kids. She liked the idea and wanted to name the girl Ana, after a school teacher friend of hers and I named the boy Marcus after a basketball buddy of mine from college."

Dr. Bob knew that William was struggling with his wife Rose's death and wanted to be supportive. Then he spotted the two Security guards rushing to the area, ready to deal with the problem. Dr. Bob held up his hand to slow them down and call off the alarm. Then he motioned them to continue on toward William and he.

"William, now that you know your 'kids' are fine, will you please go home. I am sure the rest of your family will be concerned why you have not returned. I tell you what I will do. I will drive you home personally." He vowed.

"Yeah that will make everything wonderful again." William said with a chuckle that made the two guards laugh as well.

Dr. Bob did not appreciate his gesture of kindness being mocked but felt that if it helped William heal, then his ego could take the jibe. He grabbed William by the arm and once he was on his feet, he collected William's coat and turned to address the sarcastic Wolf Biologist.

"Well, now that you have mocked me, are you ready to go home or would you rather apply for a position at the Medieval Times as the Court Jester?"

William caught the sarcasm that was thrown back at him and stood there as if he were pondering which option to choose. Dr. Bob was confused by William's hesitation at first but the guards' laughter made him realize that William had yet again gotten the best of him.

"Very funny, Dr. Hearth! Now come on and let's get you home." Dr. Bob said in a curt tone to let everyone know that he did not appreciate being the butt of a joke.

Dr. Bob led William out of the zoo and to his car. After the two men sat in the seats, Dr. Bob put his keys in the ignition and turned to address William.

"You will feel better when I get you home. After all, 'Home is where the heart is' as they say."

"Not anymore." William whispered under his breath as Dr. Bob drove him home.

(AT HOME IN ROSE'S
ART STUDIO)

William meandered about in Rose's art studio just trying to 'feel' her presence. He was not in denial of her death but just did not want to accept it. He picked up a paint brush that he remembered seeing her use and held it in his hand as he aimlessly walked around. He looked at her paints, canvases and various other artistic tools but the one object that consumed his attention was the painting that was sitting on the easel where she had worked on her latest project.

He sat down in front of the painting and stared at what he saw on the canvas. All he could make out were a bunch of semi-wavy lines that ran horizontally on the canvas. There was no picture to see, at least he didn't think so. Procedures and processes were his intellectual tools, Rose had always used Imagination to write her own procedures and this was a concept beyond William's understanding. He did not fault her for her beliefs. In fact they added to her beauty. It gave him a mystery to figure out and loved her for it but at this moment he really found himself upset with the arrangement because now he was unable to relate to his wife's work. He did not enjoy being at a loss for interpretation.

The frustration inside him began to build but before it could erupt, his train of thought was disrupted by Sally Hayes. Sally was a sculptor and best friend to Rose, which meant that she was someone who understood art and could best help him figure out what the meaning of the 'painting' was and she was most welcome.

"Sally, come here and let me show you something." William said.

"William, what are you doing in here? Your guests have been looking for you for some time now. You barely spoke to them when

Dr. Bob dropped you off. Then you performed another vanishing act and I find you in here? People are already wondering if you are going to be all right. What should I tell them?" Sally asked

"Tell them that the buffet is closed and that they can all leave as quickly as they came." William said with a stern gaze in Sally's direction.

"Hey now, ease up on all of the vinegar toward me. I have known you far longer than most of those people and I know when you are blocking your feelings." Sally said in a manner that threw the hostile tone right back at him. She was a person of strong will and would not back down from a fight and William knew this too.

He stared at her, then gazed down at the floor, softened his expression and looked back at her. He did not really intend to be that mean to her but a little of the ire that had built up inside of him just oozed out.

"I'm sorry, Sally. You are right. I'm just . . . . just . . . . here without her and I just don't know where 'here' is anymore."

"I know you are hurting William but your family and friends are here too. Do not push us away because all we want to do is help, in any way possible." Sally's gaze had softened by now too and she hoped that William was finally opening up. She moved closer to him and remembered his words to her as she entered the studio.

"William, did you say you had something to show me?"

"Yes, I did! Come here and look at this painting." William insisted and held out his hand to lead her to the chair where he had been sitting, directly in front of the unfinished work.

Sally sat down slowly as she took in what she saw on the virtually blank canvas. She squinted at first as she examined the lines on the 'page'. Then as she followed the lines with her hand, without touching the painting, her eyes widened as if she had discovered the meaning of the entire work of art.

William watched as her expressions changed and when he saw her eyes light up, he could not wait to hear what she had discovered. He began to feel the urgency building up inside him and finally, he had to release it.

"Well, what does it all mean?!"

Sally sat back in the chair and reclined a bit, still looking at the painting. She had heard William's question but wanted to finish the thought in her mind before sharing it with him.

"I don't know?"

"WHAT? No, you have to know something! I watched you as you examined it and I saw your eyes go from dim to light. You may not know the whole answer but you can give me an idea about what was going through Rose's mind!"

"Okay . . . all right. First, tell me what you see here." Sally requested.

William had been behind the painting and when she asked him the question, he moved to look at Rose's work again to see if he could figure out the answer that Sally had just discovered. However as he gazed intently at the painting, he still could not for the life of him get any meaning. All he saw were semi-crooked lines crossing a would be painting.

"I don't see anything, except the odd lines and they tell me nothing, except maybe Rose started this painting sometime well into her treatments and by that time her mind was not working right because of the Chemotherapy."

"No, I was there with Rose too and if there was one thing in this world that she loved just as much as you, it was her art. Also, these lines are dry."

"So, paint dries. Big deal!" William said shrugging his shoulders.

"It is a bigger deal than you think. These are oil based paints. They take weeks to dry. Rose started this painting a few weeks ago and she just never got to finish it but I would say that this would have been her final piece."

"That's it? That is all you have to tell me? The lines are a few weeks old." William said impatiently.

"Hold your horses. I'm getting to the good part, besides I do not really know a lot about this form of art. My expertise is in Sculpture. Paintings were not . . . . 'hands on' enough for me. But what I did learn from Rose about her art was that this was the way she began every work of art, with the lines. Lines are a key concept to drawing and painting and these lines do tell a bit of a story."

"What story could that be?" William asked like a little kid begging someone to finish a bedtime story.

"Look at these lines at the top of the page and tell me what you see." She said as she pointed.

William was already in front of the painting but he repositioned himself on a box because there was no other chair next to Sally to get a better view of her interpretation of the work of art. He stared intently at the lines she indicated. Sally waited patiently for him to answer.

"I see . . . I see . . . . lines on a picture. I still don't know what they mean anymore than I did. Can you please just give me your opinion and stop trying to educate me. I am sorry if I seem rude but I just want the answer and I don't know the formula to get it." William said exasperated.

"Okay William. I am sorry. I have the instincts of a teacher and I did not mean to frustrate you even more."

"I am fine. Just please tell me." He pled impatiently.

"Well, what I see here with these lines is the sky or the horizon. Look at how close they are to each other. They run the width of the picture and they are not straight. They have a kind of slight wave about them as they flow across. Now, this could be sunrise or sundown, I don't know because there is no color as of yet. Do you understand what I am saying?"

"As a scientist I want to say 'Yes'. But I am at a loss." He said with a quiver of worry in his voice.

"Do not fret. Equate this explanation to you telling me about some sort of scientific process, I would have trouble with that too. Just as you are a scientist and you are trying to grasp an artistic process."

"Okay, just keep going." William assured her.

Sally could tell that her words had helped William and she continued on with her explanation.

"The next lines down are further apart and they have more of a sharp up and down motion to them, almost like what you might see on a heart monitor."

"More horizon?" He asked.

"No, this I believe is the background. Maybe mountains or trees but in the distance because the lines still continue across the portrait."

"Well, then what do these lines at the bottom mean? They start out straight but quickly decline down the page and just get curvier as they descend. What are they?"

"Ah, that I believe is the subject or subjects of the entire sketch. These lines differ the most from the others and you can tell she spent a bit more time on them because they are a bit bolder or darker. Whatever that was going to be would have been the subject of the work. I am certain."

"Is there any way to find out what that might have been?" William asked pleading for more understanding.

Sally leaned back in her chair and put her fist up to her mouth trying to recall every conversation she had with Rose about her work. She began to gently rock back and forth in the chair as if she were trying to coax an answer out of her mind. Then she froze in mid rock. William noticed the stoppage of movement and knew she had remembered some grain of truth that might be helpful.

"What is it Sally? I know you have something! What did you remember?"

Sally rose up from the chair and began examining the minuscule sides of the canvas as she spoke.

"Rose started her projects like this with the lines but when she had the lines drawn, she then would write on one of the sides the name of the work and there it is!" She said as she pointed to the bottom right hand corner angle of the canvas.

William looked at it the word Sally had found but could not make it out. He did not want to admit his inability but felt that this was no time for pride.

"I do not know that language. I think it may be Old English or Latin but that middle letter looks more like Russian or Danish letter."

"No, it is Greek." Sally stated.

"Greek? Rose never told me she spoke Greek? How do you know for certain?"

"Well, Rose and I did go to Greece one summer in college. It was our freshman year and it was before you and she met. Rose and I did not learn the Greek Language but we did learn a few phrases to get by in the community for the time we were there."

"Well, what does the word mean?" William asked in a puzzled manner.

"The Kids."

"The Kids? We have no children of our own. I named two wolf pups at work Marcus and Ana, the names we agreed on for our children but she never saw them. I had planned this big 'Date Night' experience for us. We would have to drop by the zoo to 'pick up something' and the pups would have been in an indoor enclosure we use to process new arrivals. Then, I would have let her see them and wait for her to comment on how 'cute' they were. That was to be the moment I would have revealed the name plate on the wall to her."

"That sounds so wonderful William. Why did you never do that for her?" Sally asked fighting back a tear.

"I . . . . I . . . . kept hoping she would get better so I could do it as a get well gift but I failed." William said as he looked around the room. He wasn't really looking at anything in particular but he just didn't want to look at Sally because he feared that he might lose his composure again.

"She never saw them?"

"No, never but the night before she went into the hospital the last time, I did tell her what I had done and she smiled the most beautiful smile I had seen in a long time."

"Wait a minute! So, you told her about the wolves some weeks ago?"

"Yes, a few weeks maybe a month or so, I cannot remember exactly. Why is that important?"

"Don't you see? We have been under the impression that Rose had begun this work several months ago but with this new information, Rose must have started this painting when she was in the midst of great pain."

"You mean she was hurting and working on this at the same time." William confirmed.

"Yes, I am not sure that the subject was the wolves you spoke of but it does seem to fit into this oddly shaped puzzle." Sally said with a smirk of confusion.

William just stood looking at the lines on the canvas. He still could not see the wolves, the land or the horizon that he desperately wanted. All he could see were the lines that had been painted. He felt as though he had missed another chance to talk to Rose and tell her how he felt. Sally looked at William and could feel the desolation growing inside of him. She moved to him and put her hand on his shoulder.

"William, stop torturing yourself. Come on back into the house with your family and friends and I will fix you some tea. You need to remember that you are still among the living now and not wallow in regrets that you cannot join you wife in the land of the deceased."

(IN THE HOUSE)

William moved purposelessly to his reclining chair in the den. He flopped down and put his face in his hands. He looked up for a moment to find Sally but she had gone to get him the tea she had promised. He shook his head and buried it once again in his hands. He was beating himself up inside because he had not understood Rose's work. He felt that she had tried to communicate with him and he was not smart enough to comprehend what she had tried to say. He so wanted to talk with her to find out what she wanted but he really knew deep down inside that he just wanted to hear her voice and feel her touch.

He sat in his chair distraught and lost in a war raging inside himself. He felt like he was having a bad dream but knew he wasn't. He put his hands up to his face and he just wanted to be alone. Then he began to feel an odd presence. He could feel someone's eyes watching him. He looked up from the chair and saw several people staring back at him. Some of the people were in tears, some just tried to look away so that they could say they did not see a grown man cry but others just stared at him with looks so sad and full of compassion. However compassion from strangers was not something William cared for at the moment.

William got up from his chair and stormed out of the room. He couldn't stand the sound of another person wishing him their condolences. He just now needed to find a place in his own house to get some peace and quiet. The only place he felt that he could get some privacy would be his study. William pushed through the crowded hall and finally arrived at his study's door. As he opened it and entered, he remembered giving someone the key and telling them to lock this door but evidentially they had failed. He closed the door behind himself and proceeded to look about the room. Nothing in his study had been molested in any way. It was just the way he had left it the last time. Then he caught a glimpse of the place that he spent countless hours working out some of his most complicated theories, his desk.

As William approached his desk, he happened to look out of the window that was directly behind his desk. The view was of Rose's studio. As he stared out of the window, he let his mind flood with memories of standing in that very spot and watching her from a far. When she had been working in the studio in the past, William got quite the show. Rose would have music of all kinds blaring about her work room and sometimes she would dance. Other times she would sing and one time in particular he saw her do a cartwheel. He wasn't sure what was happening but after she finished her 'performances' she would have very elaborate works of art to display. Rose's methods were vastly different from his own but he felt that was part of what made him love her.

William stood there just relishing the memory until he felt another well wisher's presence. This intrusion halted his stroll down memory lane and he was not happy. In a burst of anger, he turned quickly to address the trespasser.

"WHAT ARE YOU DOING . . . . " William's sentence was never finished. He was frozen behind his desk clutching his chair.

The person he had turned to yell at was not another mourner. In fact it was his wife Rose. She stood before him just in front of the closed door. She did not move nor did she speak. All she did was stand in front of him wearing the white cotton dress that she always wore when she was working in her studio. They stood there looking at each other. He tried to speak but nothing came out of his mouth because he was processing fear and elation all at the same time. His mind could not decide which emotion to experience. Then Rose tilted her head slightly in a flirtacious manner, smiled and caused William's heart to flood with elation for the first time in months.

William released the chair from his grasp and moved to embrace Rose. Tears of joy began to stream down his face as he approached her. He could not believe what was happening. His wife had not died! He must have been the victim of a cruel nightmare and now it was over. He threw open his arms to embrace her and just as he got close to her, he felt a hand grab his shoulder.

All at once he was spun around in a twirl and when the spin stopped he found himself back in the den. He frantically looked around for Rose, calling out her name but he could not find her. He then saw Sally standing before him with tears in her eyes and he felt a strong hand grab hold of his shoulder.

"Who do you think you are putting your hands on me!?" William shouted.

"I am your brother, Malcolm! And I will be the guy who knocks you out cold if you don't stop acting like a madman!"

"What do you mean? What are you saying? Where is Rose?"

Malcolm relaxed his grip but steeled his gaze as he spoke to William.

"William, Rose is dead. Any doubts you have about that fact should have been answered at the viewing. Now, what exactly are you talking about?"

William looked around the room at the looks of shock and sorrow that were displayed on the mourners' faces as they watched him.

"I am not crazy! I just saw her!" He said defiantly.

"Okay, William. Where did you see her?" Malcolm asked.

A sense of hope filled William as he began to tell his story.

"I was in my study, behind my desk and I heard someone behind me. I turned around to see who it was and there was Rose!"

"William, that is impossible." Malcolm said as sensitive but as firm as he was able.

"Why? Because you say so?" William asked curtly.

"William, you fell asleep in the chair when I went into the kitchen to get your tea." Sally said in the most soothing voice she could muster.

William looked down at the cup of tea she held in her hand. Then he looked around at all of the faces again. The walls of reality seemed to be fading around him and he made one more defiant grasp to hold on to the new hope that he had just found.

"Wait, of course, she is not here. She was in the study! Follow me I will show you." William said and stormed out of the room and down the hall to the study.

Sally had hurried behind him as Malcolm had stayed behind to put the guests at ease. William reached the door and turned the knob to enter the room but the door was locked. He tried again and when that attempt failed, he tried to push his way into the room but found the same result.

"What is going on here?! Why is this door locked? It was just open a few minutes ago!"

"What do you mean William?" Sally pleaded.

"I was in this room until someone grabbed me by the shoulder and dragged me back to the den. In there is where I saw Rose!" William pointed as he spoke.

"William, what are you talking about?" Malcolm asked. He had heard William's continued rant as he made his way to the study.

"Rose is in the study! Why is this door locked?"

"Because you gave me the key before the funeral!" Malcolm said as he held the key out in the palm of his hand for them to see.

"So you . . . if this is locked . . . then . . . I don't . . ." William's stammer was interrupted by Malcolm's explanation.

"Don't you remember giving it to me and telling me that you 'didn't want people prodding around in your personal working space.'?"

William looked down at the key in his brother's hand and reality appeared to sink into his mind. William took the key and stared at it as if he were trying to recall everything that had happened. He couldn't get his mind straight. He used the key and made his way into the study. He rushed around the room as if he were looking for something or someone.

All Sally and Malcolm could do was look on as they watched William search. Their hearts went out to him but they knew they had to act before this scenario got worse. Sally did not know Malcolm all that well but knew she had to work with him to help her friend.

"He has totally changed since the hospital." She whispered to Malcolm.

"What do you mean?" He whispered back as they both watched William search his study.

"Before Rose got sick, he was very friendly and caring but when she got sick and right up to when they took her off the machine, he was cold as if nothing mattered."

"It's a bad time. He is just going to have to trudge through it. I will help and I hope I can count on you?"

"Of course you can. Rose had been my best friend since college. I miss her terribly and I know she would not want to see him like this."

They gave William another moment or two to canvas the room and assure himself that Rose was in fact not there with him. Then he stopped looking and just stood in the room with his back to Sally and Malcolm.

"William, come sit down with me." Sally begged.

"I know she is here! I can feel her!" William said frantically.

Malcolm moved to intercept his brother's search and grabbed him by the shoulders.

"William, listen! Rose is gone! You don't have to like it but you do have to accept it, or else you will drive yourself mad trying to find her."

"I don't have to try to find her because she is here!"

Malcolm had moved beyond compassion and was now in full intervention mode. He wanted to help his brother but his brother was completely devoid of reason at the moment. He knew that he would have to confront William's beliefs head on and break down the walls of William's fantasy world where Rose was still alive.

"Okay fine! Where would you like to look! Oh wait, didn't you say she was right here by the door? Well, I don't see her there? Maybe she is in the closet? Wow, that would be weird to find her in there!" Malcolm said as he moved toward the closet door.

Now it was William and Sally who stood by in shock as they watched Malcolm search for Rose. The difference was that when William searched, he fully expected to find his lost love and when Malcolm searched, there was a sense of mocking that hung in the room.

"Malcolm! What has gotten into you?" Sally scolded.

"Nothing or well everything! I am helping my brother search for a ghost! You should join in the search Sally. She was your best friend, I am sure you want to speak with her too."

"Malcolm, STOP! This is horribly cruel! How can you be so mean to your own brother?"

"I am not being mean. I am trying to help! You are the one who is standing around like a bump on a pickle. Join the search!"

"Oh my gosh, I am the only sane person in the room." Sally said as she sat down on the couch and put her face in her hands.

"STOP IT, MALCOLM!" William shouted.

William had ceased his search when his brother had joined in and began mocking him. All William could do was watch as Malcolm tore through the room. When William shouted, the activity in the room came to a sudden halt. Sally looked up from the couch and Malcolm dropped the empty box he had been holding. They both stared at William who now had the look of a defeated man on his face. Tears streamed down his face, red with anger. He was not really angry with his brother because his brother was just trying to show him what he had looked like. Now that he had been confronted, he was furious with himself.

"I know Rose is dead. I have no illusion about that. Everywhere I look for her she is not there. Everywhere I used to find her is now vacant. It feels as though I have had a piece of my heart ripped out and now there is a gaping wound. My heart doesn't beat right anymore. The only time I have felt normal is when I saw her in this room. Only . . . . I guess it wasn't in THIS room. I guess I was dreaming. I just want to dream again because then I will be with her." William said as he collapsed to the floor and hung his head.

Malcolm and Sally rushed to his side and helped him up. Malcolm's plan had worked and now William was ready to get some sleep. They ushered him to his room and Sally took his shoes off after he fell into bed. William went right to sleep and the concerned friends turned off the light and let him rest.

"Sally, look I want you to understand . . . . " Malcolm started to explain but Sally stopped him.

"It is okay. I admit I did think you had gone crazy but then I realized what you were doing and it worked. Just let me know before you try anymore PSYCHO Therapist tricks."

"Very well, it was a spur of the moment idea. Are you staying here tonight? My wife had mentioned something about that."

"Yeah, I have to go to France tomorrow for the opening of one of my pieces. Usually, I would stay here if I had to fly out the next day. This way I did not have to rush across town to get to the airport."

"Well, I just didn't want William to be alone tonight. When will you be back?

"I just have to be there for the opening tomorrow night. I can come home right afterwards if you think William will need someone here."

"No, my family and I will keep him company. Enjoy your trip. We will come by tomorrow and clean this place up."

"I will start the dishes and you guys can get the rest. Will he go to work?"

"I don't know but I will be here tomorrow when he wakes up just to make sure he is okay."

Sally closed the door behind Malcolm and looked at the mess of the house. She couldn't believe that high society people could be so messy. She moved to the kitchen and began working on rinsing the dishes before she put them in the dishwasher.

Washing dishes was a monotonous task but it had to be done. Her mind began to wander back to another time when she had helped

Rose do the dishes. They were so close that some people actually had mistaken them for sisters. Then, Sally was brought out of her nostalgic moment by the sound of someone walking the hall.

Sally thought that William had awakened and was meandering about the house. She dried her hands and walked down the hall but did not see him. She looked around and noticed that the studio light was on. She started walking toward William's room and began coming up with what to say to him. Then as she passed by his room, she could hear him snoring from the hall. She gently poked her head through the door and watched as the light from the hall slowly lit the room. She allowed just enough light in to make sure William was okay and not disturb his slumber.

Sally was surprised at what she witnessed. William was still out cold and in the exact position she had left him when she readied him for bed. William then began to tussle and she quietly and quickly closed the door. Sally knew that she had heard someone walking down the hall and she could see that the light in the studio was still shining. She pressed on to the studio.

When she reached the studio door, she noticed that it was ajar. She remembered turning off the light and closing the door and was now certain something was odd. As she moved into the studio, she checked to make sure that nothing had been molested or stolen. There were some paints moved and even used but she could not see what had been painted with them. Sally kept thinking about how spooky the whole night had been with William's episode and now what she had noticed. She knew that William did not need any more weirdness in his life and so she turned off the light and closed the door. She knew that she needed some sleep and that was what she felt had caused her odd moment.

"I need some sleep! I guess this house is making all of us a little loopy this evening." She said to herself and went to the guest room to go to sleep.

(THE NEXT NIGHT)

William had collapsed on his bed after a day of frustration. He tossed and turned for what seemed like hours and finally just lay in bed going over the day's events in his head. He woke up and Rose was not there. He had gotten ready for work and Rose was not there. He went to work trying to regain some sense of normalcy but Rose never called him like she had always done. He came home and went to see her in her studio but she wasn't there either. That was not really all that odd because she would be gone from time to time when she did not have a project that she was working on but she would always leave a note if she had not called him to tell him where she was going. He had looked in every nook and cranny of the house but he could not find her. He knew he was not crazy. He had accepted that she had passed away but that still did not stop him from wanting her to be there.

William could not lay there any longer. He got up and stumbled to the bathroom. He felt his way to the sink and didn't even bother to turn on the light. He ran some water in the sink and let it wash over his hands, then cupped up some and splashed it on his face. With his faced soaked, he grabbed for a towel. In his blinded search, he had inadvertently turned on the mirror light at the sink. He finally found the towel and wiped every drop from his face hoping that the towel had absorbed the misery that he had felt. Then he might be able to sleep.

William looked at himself in the mirror as the bluish light made him appear like a Smurf. He choked back a laugh but then noticed another shape behind him in the mirror's reflection. He leaned into the mirror to make the image clearer and then realized what it was.

He spun around to make sure his suspicion was correct. There behind him in the doorway stood his departed wife Rose.

William did not know whether to scream in fear or cry in elation so he stood staring at her in silent shock. He just wanted to look at her and she stood in front of him smiling in her white work dress. Finally, he gained the courage to speak.

"I must be dreaming but I don't care. I just want to be with you. If this is a dream, I don't want to wake and if this is real I don't want to sleep."

Rose stood in the door way and smiled as if she were happy to hear him say he missed her. Then she moved toward him and gave him a very gentle kiss on his lips. It seemed to rid him of his apprehension but not his confusion.

"Rose, why am I seeing you? Please, help me understand." He begged.

She smiled more and then held up one finger and motioned him to come to her. William did not need any more encouragement and eagerly moved toward her but as he neared, she moved away.

"Rose, what are you doing? Where are you going?"

She held up the same finger but this time put it to her lips in order to tell him to stop asking questions. William stood confused for a moment but then just obeyed her request and followed her. Rose strolled down the hall to her studio as William rushed to catch up to her but try as he may he could never catch up. Finally, they arrived at her studio and she stopped to wait for him.

"Rose, how are you able to move so fast?"

She did not answer him but pointed to the studio door. William looked at her confused.

"Aren't you a ghost? Why don't you just walk through the door?"

Rose's expression changed to an impertinent frown as if she were not amused with his wry sense of humor. Then she pointed at the door like a mother would point to send her child to his or her room. William chuckled a bit but relented and opened the door. He waited for her to enter but she motioned for him to go on into the room. After he had made it into the room he turned to look for her. She wasn't there anymore.

"Rose? Rose! Where are you?" William shouted as he frantically looked around to find her. Then out of the corner of his eye he caught sight of her at the painting she had started.

"Don't you scare me like that! I thought I had lost you again. Why are we in here?"

Rose did not answer him but just continued to work on her painting. William gave up trying to talk to her because he knew that when she was working, she would not talk until she had finished. Then it hit him. That was why she was not speaking to him because she had a project to finish. William nodded in agreement with his hypothesis, as he moved closer to her to see what she was doing.

William did not want to disrupt her, so he took a position standing behind her where he could get a clear view of her work. There was something familiar about the painting. The lines looked similar to the painting she had started before she died but why would she work on that painting? What made it so special? He watched as she diligently worked on the canvas but after watching her for a bit, he could not keep his head up and fell asleep trying to watch.

A sharp pain shot through William's back and made him wake up. He looked around for Rose but could not find her. He looked in the bed beside himself and then he leaned up to look into the bathroom but could not find her. He realized something really strange. He was in his bedroom, but he distinctly remembered falling asleep in a chair in his wife's art studio.

William leaped out of his bed and ran down the hallway to the studio. He opened the door and went into the room. He still had yet to find Rose but moved to the painting she had been working on last night in the dream. He stared at the painting in disbelief. He knew last night he had been dreaming and was grateful for it but the work his wife had been attempting to complete, in the dream, he now stared at on the canvas. He could not for the life of him figure out what was happening. How could what happened in a dream come true in reality? Maybe it wasn't a dream? He rubbed his face with his hands in a vain attempt to push some sense into his head. Then he ran back to his bedroom and got his cell phone.

William sat on the edge of the bed and tried to think of someone to call to tell this story. Then he remembered that Sally had spent the night, to watch over him. He ran down the hall and threw open her door but she was not there. He found a note on the bed that explained that she had to take a redeye flight and had left before he had awakened. He thought for a minute and decided to see if her flight had left so he called her cell. William then happened to look at the calendar, then he checked the date on his phone and realized that the note he was reading was a couple of days old. He thought for a moment and began dialing her number. The phone rang and then rang again and again, William started to hang up but then he heard her answer. William explained the entire situation to Sally on the phone and anxiously awaited his friend's opinion.

"I know this is all a bit weird but I just need some sort of understanding." William begged

"And you called me? I am not a psychiatrist or a psychic! I don't know what to make of it all."

"Really? Not even a guess?"

"William, I . . . I will be back in town in a couple of days. Perhaps we can talk then okay? Maybe you should call your brother? He would know better than me."

"I thought about that but I just think that he would tell me I was crazy or that I was distraught or something like that but I know what I felt and I know what I saw! It happened!"

"Okay! Okay! I have to go now but I will talk to you again and soon." Sally assured and then hurriedly ended the call.

William sat on his bed and wondered what to do. Then he gave up and just got dressed for work. There was just too much going on for him to understand. Maybe throwing himself into his work was the tonic he needed.

(A COUPLE OF DAYS LATER)

William slammed a book shut as if he were angry with it and threw it against the wall. He argued with himself as he muttered under his breath unbeknownst that his brother had entered his office.

"Have I come at a bad time brother?" Malcolm asked with a hint of scorn in his voice to heap some shame on his brother about the outburst.

William turned and shot a nasty look of contempt back at Malcolm. William regained his composure, picked up the book he had just thrown and sat down behind his desk. He opened the book and pretended to ignore his brother. He stared at the book but he was not reading it and finally he answered the question.

"No, what gave you the idea that you had come at a bad time?"

"Well, the temper tantrum I just witnessed did not exactly make me feel welcome."

William fought back the urge to laugh and continued to look at the book. Then he cleared his throat and looked up from the book for a second and then went back to 'reading'.

"Well, Malcolm consider yourself, welcome."

"Oh, stop pretending to read! The book is upside down!"

"WHAT DO YOU WANT, MALCOLM?" William yelled slamming the book in question on the table.

"I want you to . . . . " Malcolm started to say calmly but was interrupted angrily.

" . . . tell you what is bothering me? So you can shrink me? No thanks!" William said.

There was a moment or two of silence between them as they sat and stared each other. Malcolm took a deep breath and tried to get through to his brother again.

"William, I can see you are hurting. It hurts me to see you like this."

"Well, how about I just smile when I am around you and then you won't have to see me in pain? Maybe then you will feel better!"

"Smile all you want but I know you are in pain and if you will just knock that chip on your should off for a minute, you will see that I, and everyone else, are just trying to help you. I meant to stop by the next day after the funeral and check on you at your house but I got busy. My wife, my kids and I have tried to call you several times, I knew you would not answer but we tried anyhow."

William started to respond in anger once more but stopped himself before he could get the words to pass his lips. This time he made the sigh and it appeared that just as the air left his lungs, a bit of his anger fled too. He looked across the table at his brother and then looked back down at his desk. He cleared his throat and took a big breath through his nose and relaxed.

"I . . . I am not sleeping well."

"I can see that. I can give you something to help you get to sleep if you want?" Malcolm asked.

"That's just it, I can get to sleep but even after I have slept for nine or ten hours, I wake up only to feel as though I have not gotten enough sleep."

"It is stress William. It will pass. That is what the meds are for. They help you over the proverbial hump."

William sat up in his chair and looked away from Malcolm. He had something he wanted to say but was not really sure how to tell his shrink brother and not get committed. Malcolm could sense that William had a secret that he was protecting.

"Is there something you are not telling me, William?" Malcolm asked cautiously.

"I know you are not going to believe me but I know this happened!" William said forcefully.

"What happened, William?" Malcolm said in a concerned manner.

William hesitated to respond. He shuffled papers around his desk as if he were looking for something and had a nervous look on his face. He struggled for the words to tell his brother what he was feeling. He knew Malcolm wouldn't believe him but he wanted him to understand. Finally, William stopped fidgeting and let out a deep sigh. He sat up in his chair and cleared his throat.

"I don't know if I want the stress to clear."

Malcolm was stunned by his brother's declaration. He leaned back in his chair across from William and tried to quickly and cleverly come up with a response that would help his brother. Now, it was Malcolm whom did the fidgeting. For the life of him, Malcolm could not figure out a response. And when a therapist reaches that place in a session, all he or she can do is hope for the best.

"William, why would you want the stress to continue? Why would you want the pain to continue? Please help me understand I am concerned for your safety. This stress will kill you if you allow it to and I do not want that to happen to you!" Malcolm said almost choking up.

"I'm not saying I want to die. Nor am I saying that I'm going to cause myself harm. Ever since Rose's funeral, something has been happening to me . . . . "

"Yes, William it is called grief!" Malcolm interrupted.

"No, dang it, that is not it! Will you let me finish my sentence?" William said angrily as he stared at his brother. William paced about behind his desk for a moment and allowed his anger to subside.

"I have never felt like Rose has left. I have always felt that she is still here with me and I know that sounds crazy but I can honestly say that I feel her presence, especially when I dream."

"William, that doesn't sound crazy at all. In fact, if my wife had died, I would certainly want to feel as though she was here with me."

"There is more to it than that, Malcolm." William insisted.

"Well, what exactly are we talking about?"

"It is the painting . . . the last painting that Rose was working on when she died."

"I had no idea that Rose made another painting? How long ago had she completed it?"

"She didn't. She began working on it after she was diagnosed and it appears that she began working on it after she had started her treatments."

"How could she have worked on it? She would've been in excruciating pain. Perhaps she could have made a few stray lines on the canvas but nothing like her previous work."

William had been looking down at his desk but when he heard his brother's explanation, he snapped his head back to look at Malcolm.

"Well . . . that is how the painting started!"

"I feel a 'but' coming on William." Malcolm said curiously.

"For the past couple of nights, I have been dreaming about Rose and she has been painting."

"Well that's nothing odd. You were dreaming about her in a manner in which you saw her regularly and that is her working."

"This is different!" William insisted.

"How is this different?"

"Because in my dream she is painting and . . . . talking to me . . . . and in reality the painting IS getting completed!" William said and set back in his chair as if he had proven a point.

"Wait a minute! Are you telling me that your dreams are coming true?!"

"Yes, they are in a matter of speaking because whatever happens in my dream is completed on that canvas. I see Rose painting in my dream and when I go look at the paining, it is filled in more."

Malcolm tried to hide the confused and horrified look on his face. He was no longer afraid that William was going to hurt himself or anyone else but now he was concerned for William's sanity. It was one thing to have similar events happen in a dream and have them happen in reality, that maybe attributed to happenstance but here William was now telling him that he had been communicating with a spirit and that the spirit is influencing his life. Malcolm took a deep breath and then let it out slowly before he responded.

"Okay William . . . I know you love and miss your wife and you want her to still be a part of your life but if you go around telling people that your dreams are coming true, they are going to start doubting your sanity. Surely you've misinterpreted what you saw. Perhaps the painting was more done than you thought when you first saw it and after your dream, you took the deeper look at the painting and notice more detail to it?"

"No, I even got to Sally to look at the painting before she left for Europe. She is the person who told me about the lines. She told me the meaning of the lines and what Rose was trying to portray with the painting."

"William, I understand this is stressful and I appreciate the fact that you've gone through a great loss. You should know that for the next few months you will be more sensitive to everything than you ever have been. This is the point where many people, be they survivors of a crash of some sort or . . . . those who have lost their mate, find themselves in harmful situations. They sometimes feel as though they want to go back to before the event happened that changed their lives and they will try to do any and everything they can alter what happened. But what eventually happens to them, is the reality they are wishing for, never comes true and they are left with a huge hole where their heart was and for most, this reality is too much to bear."

"You said most, not all. What happens to the rest?" William asked matter-of-factly.

"What do you mean?" Malcolm asked.

"I mean all that bull you just said about the gaping hole in people's hearts and not being able to recover. Then you went on to talk about 'for most the reality is too much to bear' not all. What happens to the rest of them?"

"The rest of them . . . William, listen to yourself! You are grasping at straws trying to hang onto something here that is desperately trying to let you go. I know this is terrible but you have to move on, you have to LIVE!"

William's face turned blood red, boiling with anger. He felt as though his brother was trying to get him to forget about the love of his life. However, William had already exploded in anger at the beginning of this impromptu meeting and he did not want to give his brother the satisfaction of being right about anything. So, he sat back down in his chair and cooled off by taking a sip of water from a cup on his desk. He cleared his throat and by this time, his anger had relaxed yet again.

"I am trying to move on with my life. I know what I saw in my dream and I know what I saw on the painting."

Malcolm could see that he was reaching his brother. He could also see that William had just fought back some rage. Malcolm knew he had to tread lightly. He thought for a moment and then came up with a possible solution.

"Okay William, the painting was one way when you went to sleep and then it was different when you woke up, am I right so far?"

"Yeah, where you going with this?" William asked cautiously.

"Bear with me here. I think I found the solution. Now, I think we're both right. Let me explain. You say you saw something in a dream and then it happened in reality. I say that can't happen but you swear that it did. Now, what if your dream was just as you said but instead of the dream coming true, something else affected the painting."

"Okay . . . . what else could there be? Are you telling me that you believe me?"

"Not exactly but here is what I do believe is happening, you saw what you saw in dreamland and then someone else worked on the painting. That way when you woke or the next time you looked at the painting, you would see what you wanted to see or what you saw in your dream."

"Okay but who would do that?"

"William, you said yourself that you have been dreaming this for a while. I am certain that you told other people. In fact I know that you told Sally by your own admission. Is she not an artist?"

"Yes, she is an artist but she is a sculptor not a painter."

"I see and I suppose it was she who told you that she was not a painter."

"As a point of fact she did. Why does that matter?"

"William, she was Rose's best friend and I'm sure she wants to spare you any harm at all but I get the feeling that after you told her this dream she then got into your house and worked on the painting. Of course she would tell you that she's not a painter, that way it would throw you off the scent and you would never suspect her because she is the most likely suspect. I think she is trying to give you a very sweet gift, a way to remember her friend and your wife. My advice to you is to continue with your dreams and just let them take you where they will and as for Sally, continue to update her on your dreams and never let her know that her secret is out, at least until the painting is complete. At that point, all will be well and you can look back and laugh . . . and perhaps have one last cry. And then move on with your life."

William put his hand on his head as if checking himself for a fever. Malcolm's words rang true. It was a sweet gesture that Sally was trying to make and a great expense for her. Sally would have gone to Europe and then come back home secretly the very next day in order to give herself an alibi and then carefully sneak into the house to work on the painting.

"This would have taken months of planning. How could she have done this alone?" William asked.

"You said it yourself brother, it would've taken months. Perhaps, she and Rose got together and formed this little plan for you. I don't exactly know how they get you to dream what you dreamed but perhaps there were enough subtle reminders throughout the house and perhaps a few carefully worded reminders by Rose before she died and Sally before she left for Europe."

"I don't . . . . I don't see how this is possible?" William said dumbfounded.

"I told you that you are going to be sensitive to things in a way that you have never been before. You will pick up meanings in conversations, clouds in the sky and writing on the wall like you wouldn't believe. This is what I mean when I say you must be careful during this time. Just let Sally do this and just get on with your life, okay. When the women in your life have gathered in their minds to do something for you, my advice is to let them. Trust me you'll be better off."

William and Malcolm shared a laugh on that note. The moment of levity had done them both some good, especially William. They both leaned back in their chairs and let out a big sigh of relief. Then all at once, William sprang to his feet, tidied up his desk and started to walk out of his office. Malcolm rose to his feet quickly and tried to keep up.

"William, where you going?"

Without stopping, he gave Malcolm a response.

"You said I should go home, well I'm going to take that advice. Maybe I can even catch 'someone' in the act and then I can find the truth."

"Good luck, William and be gentle with her. It is a sweet gesture."

(AT HOME)

William hurried home with great anticipation. His hope was that he could catch Sally in the act and make her admit to her plan. He was not upset with her but was more relieved that he was not 'haunted' or insane. He thought Sally's gesture was nice but she really should have talked with him about it before she put the plan into motion.

The car creaked to a halt as quietly as William could make it. He had stopped the car at the end of the driveway because from that point, his approach would be covered by a hedge that lined the lane leading up drive way. William peeked through the bush to see if he could catch a glimpse of Sally in the house but even as hard as he looked, he could not find any trace of her. He knew that she had said that she was to still be in Paris at the time but that was of course her 'official' story and he was too smart to fall for that . . . . again.

William crouched down and crept along the hedge that led up to the house like a soldier trying to infiltrate an enemy base. His mind was focused so intently on exposing and confronting Sally that an explosion could have gone off next door and he would not have noticed. He moved as quickly as he could in the crouched position and finally reached the side of the house that completely concealed his presence. He continuously peeked around each corner trying not give away his position. Finally, he had made it to the outer door of Rose's Studio and gingerly poked his head to the edge of the window and peered into the room.

The only thing that William knew about Sally's work ethic was that she liked to work quietly. Unlike Rose, who played music and even danced while she worked, Sally just put her mind into her work and ignored the world. William saw this trait as a good and a bad characteristic. It was good because she would be oblivious while she worked and he would be able to easily sneak up on her but then again because she was so quiet, he was unable to tell from a far if she was working. William glanced to the left and then to the right but could not see Sally. He had a perfect view of the painting but there was no one in the room.

William was a bit disappointed but then consoled himself with the notion that maybe Sally had already finished working on it for the day and even perhaps that Malcolm had called her and told her that he was on the way and she quickly escaped. He wondered if any of his movements had been caught on the cameras or if his neighbors had seen him. They may have even been concerned that he was a burglar.

"HOLD IT RIGHT THERE, BUDDY!" a voice behind William shouted and he froze in fear. He had no idea who this could be but feared that he may have stumbled into a burglary. He had been carrying his shoes in his hand but the shout caused him to send them flying in opposite directions.

"Now, put your hands up high in the air and slowly turn around." The voice commanded.

William was scared out of his mind by this point but just as his fear was about to get the best of him, he saw who was threatening him. The Police Officer still had a gun pointed at the quivering scientist but William knew that he was not about to get robbed but he now feared that he might have to go to jail. He had not heard the officer pull up behind him but definitely heard him now.

"Officer, this is my house. I know it may not look that way . . . . and I do not know who called or what story you were told but this is my house." William assured him.

"Do you have some form of identification on your person, Sir?" The officer asked in the very direct manner that he was trained.

"Identification . . . Yes! Yes, I DO!" William said excitedly and urgently reached for his wallet that he kept in his pocket.

"SLOWLY, SIR!" The officer yelled and made William freeze as if he were playing a very odd game of 'Red Light, Green Light' with the Policeman.

Both men's hearts were racing by this time but William's heart was in his throat. William kept one hand in the air and turned to reveal his rear pocket to the officer to assure him of what he was reaching for and finally, he was able to produce his identification.

Now, both men took a deep sigh of relief and a calm came over the situation. The officer looked at the license and then back at William. The officer holstered his weapon and returned to his car. William slumped down on a small bench that was by the outer door to the studio. He then took a quick glance into the studio again and to his surprise, he saw the outline of someone approaching the outer door from inside the studio. William turned his body so that he could get a full look at the person approaching the door. He began to make out a female shape and then he could not believe who he saw standing there. It was Rose.

"Okay, Sir! Here is your ID back." The officer said to William and made him jump with a great fright.

"Sir, are you feeling well?" The policeman asked William.

William looked at the concerned policeman and then looked back to the studio. Standing in the door way, keeping the door a jar with her body was a very shocked Sally.

"William . . . . what on Earth is going on here?!" She said.

"Madam, do you know this gentleman?" The policeman said to Sally.

"Yes, he lives here. I just stopped by to check on him."

"AHA! So, you were here!" William shouted with a large grin on his face.

"Yes, William. My plane got in early and your brother called me and I came right over."

William crossed his arms and looked at her out of the corner of his eye to show his disbelief of her story.

"Oh, you JUST got here?" William said wryly.

"Yes." Sally said not sure of where William's suspicion was coming from.

"And your plane . . . from Europe . . . came in early?"

"Yes."

"Oh and this is my favorite (William said as grabbed the officer by the arm with his left hand and held up his right finger as he spoke.) My brother called you and told you I was home or on my way home."

"Yes, William. What is with all of the questions?"

William scoffed and looked at the police officer like he was letting him in on the joke. The officer was not amused and just looked at William grimly and then lowered his gaze to William's grasp of his arm. Then he looked back up at William even more grim. William understood the officer's expressions and released his arm as quickly as he could. The officer then turned to Sally.

"Madam, what exactly did this man's brother tell you?"

"Yes, that is an excellent question and you have to answer truthfully because you are under oath!" William said in a matter of fact way.

"No, she's not." The officer informed William.

"Well, she can't lie . . . because you can take her to jail!"

"No, I can't."

"Then what good are you?!" William yelled frustrated.

"Madam, do you wish me to take this man with me?"

"No, officer. I just got a call from his brother that William and I need to discuss."

"What is his brother's occupation?"

"He is a Therapist?"

Now, it was the Officer's turn for a moment of discovery. He turned to William and pointed.

"Aha! Now, we get the truth. Things are starting to make sense for once today."

William was stupefied and he was again afraid of being carted off to jail or worse.

"No . . . . well he is . . . but I am sane. As a matter of fact I just had a talk with him and he said I should go home. Not, because I am unstable but so I can catch the person who was in the house."

"Who lives here with you? Your wife?" The officer asked.

"No, yes, well . . . my wife lived here with me . . . . but then she died."

"Did she die in this house?"

"No, in my arms . . . . in the hospital . . . of Cancer!" William said flustered.

"Officer, I assure you everything is fine. William is a well noted biologist at the local zoological gardens and he is going through a period of adjustment right now because of his wife's passing." Sally said.

"Okay, why didn't he just say that?" The officer asked and pointed to William.

"Well, I did . . . or would have . . . . I mean what she said was good . . . . it has been a weird day." William stammered.

"And getting weirder it seems." The officer said sarcastically.

"Please just go, officer. I can take it from here." Sally said.

"Are you sure?"

"Yes, Sir I am. Besides if there is a problem I have your number to call."

"You have my number? What are you talking about?"

"I assume it is still 9-1-1."

"Funny." The officer said and put on his soul covering sunglasses and made his way back to his car and left.

William sat on the bench again, this time with his head down staring at the grass on the lawn. Sally walked over to him and sat beside him without saying a word. She let some time pass and then put her hand on William's shoulder.

"Having a bad day are we?" She asked.

"I don't want to talk about it. I just want to go inside and sit in my chair."

William and Sally got to their feet and walked inside through the studio door. William stole a glance from the easel that held Rose's painting. He could not see the image on the canvas from his vantage point but he had just been through a bit of an ordeal so, he just moved on through the room and into the hallway.

(IN THE LIVING ROOM)

William collapsed on the sofa in front of the television and just stared at the blank screen. He did not really want to watch anything, he was just too busy processing a feeling of relief that he was not shot or arrested, he was embarrassed at having the Police try to apprehend him on his lawn and disappointed that he had been unable to prove that Sally was in fact the person making the portrait.

"William, are you going to turn on the TV?" Sally asked as she entered the room and offered him a glass of iced tea.

"I am not thirsty nor do I care to see what is on TV?" William said rather pointedly.

"Are you too afraid that you might see yourself on the news, trying to break into your own house?" Sally asked with a smirk.

William had been just staring at the TV, caught in a blank stare but his gaze was broken when he heard Sally's sarcastic question. He turned to her and gave her a glaring look.

"No, I just don't want to . . . . " William's words trailed off because just behind where Sally was standing, he saw Rose walking down the hallway. William did not bother to finish his sentence or even tell Sally what he had seen. He just rushed to catch up with his dearly departed wife.

William rounded the corner to see Rose enter her studio and he hurried into it as well. Upon entering the studio William looked and found her right where he thought he would, at her easel working on another masterpiece.

"Rose, I am so glad to see you!" William exclaimed.

"My dear William, where else would I be?"

William wanted to rush to her and grab her up in his arms but he knew she was not really there or at least he thought she was not. His brother's words rang about in his head as his eyes and heart tried to tell him a different story. He thought for a moment then came up with the only plan he could. He strolled up to her and looked at the painting. The lines were not alone on the canvas. In fact, he could see land and sky starting to take shape. It was going to be her Magnum Opus and he could not wait to see it completed. Then he pulled himself back to reality.

"Rose, why is this happening?" William begged.

"I have to finish my work." Rose said plainly.

"I am a man of Science. I don't believe in ghosts."

"Okay. Then you are crazy because only crazy people see people who are not there or give credit for work that they didn't do."

William did not know how to respond to Rose. He stood there just looking at her and put his fist up to his mouth in an attempt to think his way out of the situation. Then he snapped his fingers to signify that he had an explanation.

"I have been under a lot of stress because of your . . . my wife's death and I have been doing everything I could to keep you . . . my wife, in my life and this is just a dream."

"So, you would let your brother convince you that I am not real?"

"No, you were real. Now, you are dead. I mean my wife is dead!"

Rose dipped her brush down in the water, cleaned and dried it with a rag. She put the brush down on the tray below the easel and moved toward William.

"I maybe dead but I am still your wife William." Rose said and kissed him on the cheek as she walked passed him.

"Wait, where are you going?" William asked.

"I can see my presence here has disturbed you and I NEVER wanted to do that. This painting was to be my gift to you but I see that I will have to go now and just leave the work unfinished. Your Science can not explain my presence because you cannot use your mind to find the truth in this situation. You must use the part of you I fell in love with, your heart. Let me know when that man wants to see me and I will come back."

When Rose finished, she began her departure again. William watched as she vanished through the door and then he heard banging on the other side of door. He was shocked. Why would Rose bang on the door if she could walk through it? He threw the question out of his mind as soon as he thought it and hurried to open the door.

"Rose?" William said as he opened the door quickly.

"William?! What on Earth are you doing in here?! You just hurried past me and did not even finish your sentence before you rushed off! I could not keep up with you and carry this tea and then I had to look all over this house to find you! I finally I heard your voice and followed it here. What are you doing in the studio?"

William wanted to tell her what he had been doing but was unsure if she would believe him or just call his brother and have him put on some type of medicated drip, strapped to a hospital bed and locked in a rubber room. William then tried to come up with a brilliant and touching story about how he was letting Rose go but he knew that probably would not work. Then he arrived at the only response he could muster with any certainty.

"Nothing. I am doing nothing in here. Just like I always did. This was Rose's room." He said as he moved slowly past Sally and on into the hallway grabbing the tea out of her hand as he passed.

Sally went on into the room and looked to see if anything had been moved or changed and to her surprise, she noticed the painting. William was right, the painting had progressed since the last time she saw it and she did not think William had the skills for this type of art. Sally could see Rose's techniques and trademarks all about the canvas but she could not figure out how the painting was being completed or more importantly, by whom.

"William . . . did you do some painting on the canvas you showed me?" Sally asked as she hastened to catch up with him.

"What . . . No, I asked you about that painting. I am not a painter or drawer or anything of the like, that was Rose's area, she did the work. I am a scientist. But science does me little good right now. Shut the door when you are done please." William said as he walked away sipping the tea and trying to come to a logical explanation for the recent events.

"Rose . . . did the work?" Sally muttered trying to make sure she heard William correctly.

Sally was unsure what had happened. She did not believe in the ghost story William had tried to tell her but she knew that it gave him some comfort. Most importantly though, she knew the painting was being completed but not by whom. Too many questions and not enough answers is all she found. She knew that she was going to have to have some help again.

(ON THE PHONE)

Sally stepped outside the front door of William's house and sat on a small bench as she dialed Malcolm's number. She was unsure what to say but knew that she had to get some help, at least with the ghost story William seemed a little happy and now his demeanor seemed to drop into a dreadful melancholy.

"Hello" Malcolm answered.

"Malcolm, this is Sally. I think there is a problem with William."

"Tell me something I do not know. What is the problem now?"

Sally began to inform Malcolm of the events that transpired when she arrived at the house. She assured him that William was okay but that he had had a mood swing that took him from hopeful to hopeless and she was not sure how it exactly happened. Malcolm listened intently and when she had finished, offered his advice.

"I think I see what is happening. Did you tell him that you were the one working to complete Rose's painting?"

"No, of course not. Why on Earth would I tell him that?" Sally said quite confused.

"Sally, it is me here. William is not within earshot, is he?"

"No, I am outside." She said as she looked around to make certain.

"Okay then, you can tell me the truth. Look, I appreciate what you were trying to do. It is a sweet gesture but I think the jig is up and it is time to come clean."

There was a dull and awkward silence on the phone between them for few moments. Then Malcolm wondered if he had been disconnected.

"Hello, Sally?"

"I am here. I am just trying to figure out what the heck you are trying to get me to say?"

"Fine, I will say it plainly. You need to tell William that you are the one finishing Rose's work."

Another moment of awkward silence ensued but this time it was broken by Sally.

"Is there a history of mental illness in your family?!" She yelled.

Malcolm had not been prepared for a shout and dropped his phone. He nearly fell out of his chair trying to catch his phone as it fell. He managed to capture it and regained his composure.

"What do you mean, Sally?!" Malcolm asked.

"You think I am the one doing this painting? I am not a painter! I am a sculptor. I admit that there is a similarity in the two art forms but I am nowhere near Rose's quality of a painter. I could not even begin to try nor would I. She is dead and any work that is not completed by her should be left in its form because if it is altered by someone else, it then loses its value as Rose's work. The only artist that can finish a work they start is the artist who began it in the first place."

"So, you are saying that you had nothing to do with the painting?" Malcolm asked concerned.

"Am I talking to myself here? I told William about the painting's possible meanings before I left for Europe. At that time, the painting was just lines on the canvas. However, today as I got a look at the painting, I can see that someone has been working on it but my question is who?"

"You were the obvious guess to me! William had been talking about the painting while you were away but I thought that you had just told him about Europe to throw him off so that you could sneak in and finish the painting?"

"NO, I was really there and like I said, I would not touch another artist's work even if I could complete it in a respectable manner."

"Then who could it be, Sally?" Malcolm asked.

"Why don't you get over here and we will discuss it with William."

"I am on my way."

(IN THE GARAGE)

Sally pressed the button that would open the garage door and allow Malcolm's car to enter. As the door raised, she stood in the garage waiting for Malcolm to exit his vehicle. Sally looked down at the framed picture she held in her hands as Malcolm neared her.

"What have you got there, Sally?" Malcolm asked.

"It is a Valentine William gave to Rose." She said as she handed it to him.

Malcolm took the picture from her and focused his attention on it as he held it in his hands. The picture was not very impressive. It was a large pinkish/reddish heart with oddly feathered wings flapping on each side and it appeared to be flying in a very dark blue sky.

"Why are you showing me this old thing?" Malcolm asked.

Sally looked at him sternly and shook her head side to side telling him 'no'.

"This was William's last Valentine to Rose. I know because I helped him make it for her last year."

"Okay, why is this important?"

"After I got off the phone with you, I got to thinking about what explanations you might suggest and I figured that you might say that is was William finishing the painting. As you can see, he has no real talent for drawing or painting. The reason Rose loved the picture was because William tried to walk in her world and give her something real. She was impressed by the meaning of the art not the picture itself. So, if William had tried to finish the painting it would not look like it does now but more like this picture here."

Malcolm listened to what Sally had said and looked at the picture again. It was not very aesthetically pleasing but it was honest. He

58

knew William had tried his hardest but this was to the best of his ability. He knew he had to see the painting at the center of the confusion.

"Take me to this painting." Malcolm insisted.

(IN THE STUDIO)

Malcolm looked over the painting carefully. He sat in the chair and examined it and then he took a couple of steps back and viewed the canvas. Finally, he approached the painting pulled it toward his body to examine it from behind. He placed the painting back in its original position and furled his brow as he stared.

Sally had been watching all of Malcolm's movements with curiosity. She had exhausted all of her investigative abilities and was open to suggestion. When she led Malcolm into the room and showed him the painting, she was hopeful that he could find something that she missed. However, as Malcolm's inspection went on, she got less and less confident in his expertise and more confident in the fact that he did not know anymore than she but he was not going to admit it to her. She allowed him to continue until he started to sniff the paints and look at them from the bottom.

"Would you like a magnifying glass detective?" She asked in a churlish manner.

"What? All of my methods are well within the guidelines of a successful detective."

"Except for the fact that you are not a detective!" Sally pointed out.

"I will have you know, that to be a good psychiatrist, one has to be a good detective as well. I recently read an article . . . . "

"Fine! Whatever! Okay, just tell me what you think is happening." Sally said harshly, not wanting to hear his explanation.

"Well, I think I need to hear more about his recent mood change."

"I will tell you again if you stop with the Sherlock Holmes attitude."

"I am just trying to figure this mess out." Malcolm declared

Sally stared back at him as if to tell him with her eyes that she was not amused. She folded her arms and stared even harder, finally she broke Malcolm's facade.

"Okay, I am as stumped as you. Happy?"

"Well, no because I want to get to the bottom of all this and help William but I don't want to put up with your ego to do it. William was a bit down in the dumps before I left for Europe but today when I got here, he seemed hopeful. Then I found him in here just a little while ago and there was no hope in his voice. It was almost as if he had given up."

"Acceptance." Malcolm plainly said.

"What?" Sally asked.

"Dogs And Bears Don't Agree."

"WHAT?!" Sally shouted in disbelief.

"Dogs and bears don't agree is a mnemonic device used to help people remember the five stages of loss or grief. You take the first letter of every stage and make a word with it. Denial, Anger, Bargaining, Depression and finally Acceptance."

"Okay, I think get what you are saying. So, you think William is on the last stage? Maybe this is good news?"

"Not so fast. Not everybody experiences the stages the same way or in the same order or even at all."

"Well, you just went from hero to goat in record time." Sally said sarcastically.

"Just think about all of the time we spent with him over the past few weeks. Did his demeanor ever fit the pattern?"

"Well, he never denied that she was dead . . . "

Malcolm snapped his fingers as if he had just thought of something and stopped Sally in mid sentence.

"Your right but he did deny his feelings about the whole situation."

"What do you mean?"

"Remember after the funeral when he had his first episode, you told me that he had been 'cold' for a while. He has always been a nice person even when we were kids but I did not pick up on his demeanor because I was just not tuned in, I am sorry to say."

"Okay how does that help us here?"

"William was denying his feelings. He probably started the grieving process when he and Rose got the news from the doctor."

"I see what you mean and he has been angry, or at least ill-tempered, here lately too. The depression just started but what about the 'Bargaining'?"

"Well . . . . The painting! The painting was his way to allow her to leave and keep her here with him. That is what this whole charade has been about, the bargaining phrase."

"No, I told you, William does not have the ability to do this kind of work! It cannot be him."

"No, it is not him. I remember a study case from my college days. There was a man who lost his wife and he would not date anyone who did not look just like or at least very similar to his dead wife. By dating these women, who were clones of his wife, in his mind, he kept her alive."

"So, what happened?" Sally asked engrossed in the story.

"Well, he was not interested in what type of person the ladies were, only their appearance and if they altered it in the slightest way he would break up with them and try to find another 'clone'."

"That is horrible."

"Well, it got worse. After about the third disappointment, he tried to pay girls to look like his wife, of course he was not dealing with the most reputable of women by that time and got into trouble with their associates. Eventually, found himself in a hospital recovering from his wounds, he told his story there and they sent him to an institution."

"Oh my and you think William would do that?"

"No, in William's situation, I am now inclined to think that he hired someone to finish the painting and told all of us that he did not know who it was. That way he could watch the painting get done and keep her alive with this ghost story. But we will have to confront him because he needs a dose of reality or else when the painting is done he will probably just wind up tearing up his house looking for Rose before . . . . " Malcolm's words trailed off as he looked at the painting.

"Before what?!" Sally asked sharply.

" . . . before he kills himself so he can be with her." Malcolm said reluctantly.

"What are we to do?"

"Have an Intervention, right now!" Malcolm said emphatically.

(IN LIVING ROOM)

William sat in the Living Room staring at the television. He was not really watching the program on the screen but really just staring at the images allowing his mind to wander. He jumped when he noticed Sally and Malcolm enter the room and sit down next to him on the couch.

"When did you get here Malcolm?" William asked.

"Oh, I have been here a little while. I was admiring your painting." Malcolm said.

"My painting? I cannot paint. Rose was the painter. It is her painting that you were admiring." William said.

Malcolm took a quick glance at Sally and she nodded back at him. Malcolm then refocused on William.

"Well, I believe it was she who began the painting but I think we all know who is completing it, William."

"What? Wait, are you telling me that you now believe that it is Rose?" William said in a shocked and confused manner.

"I believe, that you believe, the person that is painting the picture is Rose but I know who really is completing the work."

William pointed the remote at the television and pressed pause then he stared at his half cup of tea for a moment before he took a sip. He looked up from his drink to give Sally a look to make sure she was hearing this conversation too. Sally had a strange expression on her face that reflected confusion and concern, then William focused his gaze back to his brother.

"Are you feeling okay, Malcolm?" William asked.

"I am quite fine but we are not talking about me. We are talking about you."

"Quite frankly, I do not know who you are talking about?!"

"Okay, William here is the problem. We know that the painting is being completed. We know that someone, who is really with us, is doing the work. At first, I admit you had me, and I think Sally here too, going with the ghost story because I thought Sally was doing something clever but now I know that she could not have been the one because she was not here when some of the events happened. I also thought that it might be you but Sally showed me you do not have the skills to be a painter, at least not to the caliber that Rose was and to the ability it would take to finish her work."

"Thanks . . . . I think." William said trying figure out if he was just insulted.

"Anyhow, Sally and I now know who is doing the painting and while it is not being done by your hand, it is being finished by your will."

"What?" William asked a little perturbed by Malcolm's ramble and accusation.

"There is no need to get angry. In fact it is a bit romantic but the charade has come to an end because you are now starting to believe your own ruse a little too much."

"And you believe this too?!" William rose to his feet as he asked Sally.

"Well . . . . I don't really know what to believe but I do believe that Rose is not the person completing the painting."

William sat back down and put his head in his hands. He leaned his head back against the couch and closed his eyes as he spoke.

"Okay, let me get this straight, you two now believe that I hired someone to complete the painting in order to trick myself into believing that Rose was still alive? This is laughable!"

"No, what is laughable is a grown man, a doctor of science no less, believing in ghosts so much so that he employs a person who helps him fool himself! That is not only laughable but sad!" Malcolm shouted as he rose to his feet offended by William's mockery.

"I accepted your opinion not because I believed it but because I was frustrated by the fact that I could not get my mind around what was happening. But after I left the studio today, I was upset because I had a fuss with Rose and when she left, I felt so alone. I haven't felt that alone since before I met her. But now, I know what I am seeing has to be real. So, you keep your opinion and I will keep my belief."

"Now wait boys! We are here to help, not harm. There is no need to . . . "

Sally was interrupted by a loud crash coming from the backside of the house. Sally and Malcolm stood up quickly and turned in the direction of the crash.

"What was that!?" Malcolm shouted.

"That sounded like it came from the studio?" Sally said.

"Oh, that was probably the guy I hired to finish Rose's painting. I meant to tell you, I also asked him to not only paint but break a few things and do a bit of burglary while he was here." William added mockingly from his reclined position.

"We will catch your friend!" Malcolm said and hurried to the studio with Sally trailing behind him.

As they approached, they could see a silhouette moving about the studio and trying to get back out the door leading to the backyard.

"Okay Sally, I will burst through this door and grab him. You come around and cut off his escape." Malcolm explained.

"Wait, are we really going to try and capture . . . . whoever or whatever that is?" Sally asked.

"Do not tell me you are starting to believe him? It is a man not a ghost." Malcolm assured and pushed the door open.

As they both entered the room they saw the figure leave out the door. Malcolm followed behind closely, lunged and tackled the intruder on the lawn. They wrestled about for minute and finally, the prowler surrendered.

"Okay! Okay, I give!" The trespasser said.

Malcolm stood him up and kept one hand on him. He got a look at the guy and realized it was a teenager. The kid did not look like the sort that would break into people's homes and steal or vandalize. He was a clean cut youth wearing a Polo shirt and jeans. Malcolm needed some answers.

"Okay kid, what are you doing here? You do know that breaking and entering is illegal?"

"Yes, sir but I am supposed to be here." The nervous kid stammered.

"Oh, you are? Let me guess, someone paid you to be here?"

"Yes, Mrs. Rose did, in advance."

"I see and you are to just do your job and go without disturbing anyone in the house?"

"Well, yes but usually I do not have to tell them anything. They can see my work when I am finished."

"Of course, so you do this kind of work for numerous people?"

"Yes . . . . Yes I do. Why do you ask?"

"I will ask the questions here thank you." Malcolm said frowning at the young man.

The teen gave Malcolm an angry look as he rolled his eyes in order to show his contempt for what he thought would be a lecture.

"I saw that young man and quite frankly I am still considering calling the police. So, you had better be on your best behavior."

The teen lowered his gaze as he stood in front of the angry Malcolm. Once Malcolm was sure that he had the young man's attention, he continued his interrogation.

"Okay, so let us begin again. You enter this home regularly and do your 'work'?" Malcolm said as he used his fingers to accent the quotation marks.

"Yes, sir."

"And Rose, Ms. Hearth, paid you to come here and complete her work before she passed away?"

"Yes."

"Exactly how much did she pay you for this body of work?"

"Well, I got paid $20 per week and she threw in art lessons too."

"Aha! You are her student!" Malcolm exclaimed and made the young man jump back a step.

"Wait, so Rose taught you how to paint?" Sally asked. She had been present for most of the conversation but waited until she heard this piece of information before she engaged the teenager.

"Yes, madam. I had been her student for about a year. She had said that I could come here anytime, even after she died and paint. I guess I should have asked but I thought I already had permission."

Malcolm and Sally looked at each other, grinned and nodded because they had found the missing piece to a very complicated puzzle.

"Why is this so important to you all?" The teen asked.

"Well, we had been racking our brains for an explanation as to who was completing Rose's last painting and it led some of us here to some odd conclusions." Malcolm clarified.

"What do you mean?" The teen asked.

"It is simple. Rose was your teacher. She taught you how to paint and her working directly with you teaching you the skills she possessed and like any good teacher, would have left an impression on you. So, when you started working on the painting you could have picked up where she left off because you would have had the skills and knowledge of the techniques that she employed in her work and it would appear that it was as if she were still working on the painting." Sally explained as she faced Malcolm as he nodded in agreement with her analysis.

"Wait! You two think I am completing some painting of Ms. Rose's? I did not even know she was working on a painting. I only got back into town yesterday because my family and I had gone on vacation for the past month."

"Look kid we are not upset. We are relieved. You are not in any trouble. You can be honest." Malcolm assured.

"I am! Just look at the yard. Do you see how thick this grass is? It is has gotten this bad because I have NOT been here to mow it!" The teen stressed.

Malcolm and Sally looked at the tall, thick and lush grass that was growing beneath their feet. The lawn bore the resemblance of one that had not been kept up for sometime but they all had been too preoccupied with Rose's death and William's obsession to worry about the lawn. Their victory suddenly came crashing down around them. They had thought that they had finally figured out the mystery that had plagued them but now found that they were right back where they started, square one.

"Look, I am sorry for my trespassing but I just heard about Ms. Rose's death and I knew that the lessons were over but I had left a brush here that she had given me. I just wanted a little reminder of who she was and what her lessons meant to me. Here I will give it back." He said as he held out the paint stained brush in his hand.

Malcolm and Sally looked at each other as the teen explained his rationale. They were too discouraged that their theory had been destroyed to really care about his story or his offering of peace.

"Kid, you can keep the brush. Just go! You are not in any trouble. Someone will be in touch with you about the yard next week. Just go now." Sally said.

The teen did not wait around. He put the paint brush back in his pocket and hurried home. Sally and Malcolm watched him go and when he was out of sight, they turned around and stared at the house. They had thought the 'haunting' was over and done but now they knew that it was not. They made their way back to the studio to find William and begin the laborious task of thinking of another solution.

(IN THE STUDIO)

As Sally and Malcolm entered the studio they noticed that William had made it that far but was now asleep, as sprawled out in the chair as one could be, in front of the painting that had started all of the controversy.

"He looks like he has been knocked out." Malcolm said as he chuckled.

"He looks like he is out cold. I hope he gets some good sleep. How does he sleep in that awkward position?" Sally asked.

"As kids William never had trouble sleeping. In fact, I have never heard him say he has sleep trouble."

Sally noticed that the way his neck was tilted would cause him great pain when he awoke. She moved closer to him and carefully repositioned his head in a manner that he would not wake up but would relieve the tension on his neck. William shrugged off her attempt without waking and repositioned himself. Sally laughed to herself and then caught a glimpse of the painting.

"Malcolm! Get over here and look at this!" Sally said in hushed shout.

"What is the matter?" Malcolm whispered.

Sally stood and pointed at the painting in front of them. The images were clearer now even though the painting was not completed. Two wolves, detailed down to the odd heart-like shape pattern on their fur that each of them had, frolicked in a rocky forest area as the unfinished clouds and sky hovered over them. The attention to detail was astounding. The painting did not even look like a painting but more like a photograph. It was almost as if the artist had pulled the image from their memory and pasted it to the canvas. Malcolm and

Sally looked close and took note of the texture of the painting and they could smell its pungent aroma.

"I am not imagining this. You see it too, right Malcolm." Sally asked.

"Y . . . yes but how . . . . wait. This is a picture! The painter knew we were on to him and just found this print and put it here!" Malcolm exclaimed as he had solved the mystery, again.

"Oh, do shut up. I know you deal in facts and figures but there is a fact staring you right in the face! This painting is still being completed. The last time I saw this painting, it was nowhere near this close to completion. It is Rose's work! Done by her hands! I do not know how this is being accomplished but it is happening. You must accept it!" Sally insisted.

Malcolm scratched his head as he looked at the work on the canvas. He took a deep breath, held it for a moment and exhaled roughly. He rubbed his forehead as if he was checking for a fever and then leaned against a table. As Malcolm bumped up against the table, a jar of brushes toppled over and fell to the floor making a loud crash. William awoke with a start to see Sally and Malcolm standing around him.

"What . . . What is going on here? Where did that come from?" William shouted as he pointed at the painting.

"Don't you know?" Malcolm asked.

"Well, I thought you did not approve of my explanation?" William retorted.

"I . . . . don't . . . . know anymore." Malcolm said as he turned away from them both.

"Try explaining it. I might be more receptive this time." William said.

"William, what are you saying?" Sally asked.

"That is Rose's work but those wolves on that canvas could not have been painted by her."

"What?!" Sally and Malcolm said in equally shocked unison.

"Rose never saw the two wolf pups and I never took pictures of them. There is no way she could have known about the anomaly in their fur. But then . . . . who did know but me and my staff?" William said aloud as if he were trying to debate his own memory.

"Okay, this is a whole other level of weirdness that we all have just reached!" Sally exclaimed.

(IN THE DEN)

Malcolm, Sally and William were all in the den of William's home. William sat in his chair and Malcolm on the sofa. Sally paced about in front them anxiously, trying to generate a plan to deal with the new twists that had surrounded and compounded the growing mystery that had plagued them for a while now.

"Sally, please stop pacing." William pled.

"It is how I think, especially when I don't know what to think about . . . . well you know what I mean." Sally said trying to justify her odd reasoning.

"Well, have you come up with any ideas?" Malcolm asked.

"Actually . . . . no. I am still trying to process everything."

"Welcome to the club. We have matching jackets." William joked.

"Not helping." Malcolm shot back at William, while trying to quell a chuckle.

"What about you? You're the shrink! Surely you have a theory or know someone who might have a theory or maybe a ray gun?" Sally asked.

"Nice try Sally but even if he did he would not admit to it. My brother has always been the realist sort. I was more of a dreamer than he, if you can imagine that." William said in a snide manner.

"As a matter of fact, I do know someone you can call at the university. His name is Dr. Jack Watson. He specializes in these types of . . . . matters." Malcolm said as he wrote a number down on the back of a business card and gave it to Sally.

"He is your friend. You call him." Sally asserted.

"Trust me, okay. If you call him he will come." Malcolm insisted.

"Jack Watson . . . . that name sounds familiar." William said.

"I think he was in the paper sometime ago, milling about in a cemetery." Malcolm said quickly in an attempt to pacify the question and move on to another topic.

"Maybe but it seems like there is more to that name. I cannot place it right now." William said.

Sally wondered what William was thinking but she had a phone call to make. She took out her cell phone and began punching in the number Malcolm gave her. The prospect of a new perspective added to their little mystery was inviting and she felt as though there existed some type of history to Dr. Watson and Malcolm's past and she wondered what it could be.

(8:00PM)

William, Sally and Malcolm all waited for the arrival of Dr. Watson in the den. They had just finished eating a very unhealthy supper consisting of one of the metropolis's finest but greasiest pizzas. The evening had the feel of an all night cram session that they had not had since their college days. Which would have been sweet but they were missing a key member of their party and none of them could truly put that aside and to what extent they should because this was still just a little while since Rose's passing. Perhaps they all needed a little more time for mourning.

The television was playing in front of them as they sipped their tea but they were lost in thought as they sat staring at the flame crackling in the fireplace. The rain had come upon them suddenly and it brought a cold chill with it. So, the fire was just the remedy to cure the cool and wet night air.

Then all of a sudden the peace was broken violently by someone knocking on the front door. They all rose to their feet quickly spilling what was left of their beverages all about the den floor. Malcolm and Sally hastily cleaned up the mess as William attended to the door. William peered out the tiny peephole in the door to see an average sized well dressed black gentleman shaking the downpour off of his umbrella and clothes as he awaited a greeting. William looked back into the den to see if the 'cleaning crew' had accomplished their mission and they had, so now he could invite the man into his home.

"Dr. Augustus 'Jack' Watson I presume?" William said as he offered his hand in a gentlemanly gesture of welcome. The gentleman shook the last drops of rain from his clothes and turned to address William.

"Yes and you must be Dr. William Hearth?" Dr. Watson said as he accepted the man's hand.

"Welcome to my home. We are grateful that you could stop by and visit with us on such short notice."

"Think nothing of it! Actually, it is I who am grateful. It is not every day that one gets to meet, not to mention help, someone they hold in high esteem." Dr. Watson said with star struck eyes.

"Right this way sir. We have all gathered in the den. Can I offer you a beverage?"

"Thank you, no. This evening's torrential deluge has sapped my appetite for any liquid at the moment."

William ushered Dr. Watson into the den to meet Malcolm and Sally. As they entered the room, William did not get the chance to formally introduce Dr. Watson because once he caught sight of Sally, he moved straight for her.

"You must be the wonderful sculptor Sally Hayes! I am so pleased to meet you!" Dr. Watson said with a hint of giddiness in his voice.

"Yes, I am Dr. Watson. It is nice to meet you too."

"Please, everyone just call me Jack. It is a nickname I got in Graduate School because I ran to my classes like a jack rabbit."

"Hello . . . Jack. Long time no see." Malcolm said in a respectful but not exactly warm voice as he stood by the fireplace.

"Oh, yes Dr. Malcolm Hearth. You are not still sore about the class presidential election are you?" Jack asked with a big grin.

"That is it!" William shouted and everyone turned and looked to see what his exclamation was about. William did not mean to make such an outburst however, Jack's name stood out in his mind but he could not remember from where or when. Then when Jack asked the question about the election, his mind snapped like a steel trap. William noticed the shocked looks on ever one's face and knew he had to explain.

"Sorry, everyone but I have been racking my brain ever since I heard your name mentioned. It seemed so familiar and then when I heard you mention the class presidential election, I remembered that election our freshmen year." William said motioning toward Jack.

"William, what on Earth are you talking about?" Sally asked.

"That is right, you and Rose had not come to the college yet but this was an epic event. You see, there were two candidates for President of the student government, Malcolm and Dr. Wat . . . . Jack. They had a big debate the week of the election and the event was pretty even until Malcolm got impatient and started attacking character. He knew that Jack was studying Paranormal Psychology and that he even had a club of a similar nature. So, Malcolm starts talking about his charity work and hobbies and then adds a jibe about Jack's 'ghost hunting'."

"Well, that does sound a little odd, especially in an election. So, what happened?" Sally asked.

"Jack admitted to studying the Paranormal and even being an officer in the club but then he went on to talk about how his faith in a higher power gives him the strength to open his mind and examine every aspect of a situation in order to come to a conclusion based on all of the facts. 'Believing in something is a better pursuit than denying everything.' With that statement, he drew the entire crowd in and began sharing his faith. It was an amazing speech and he won the election in a landslide." William said.

"Wow, that is amazing." Sally said.

"Well, I am not an orator but I just expressed my values and they are not political props, they are my heartfelt beliefs." Jack said.

"He is right. So much so that he inspired a revival on campus. Imagine that, a modern liberal college campus with modern students all shouting 'halleluiahs' for a while. I even heard stories about a couple of professors that packed up and left the school because they did not like the opinions the students were expressing in class. I do not know if it is true but it was a rumor." William finished the story and sat down in his chair and left Jack standing in the center of the den.

"You give me too much credit. I just hold tight to my faith and let things fall where they may. It may have been I who helped to start the revival but it was The Almighty who provided the true spark in the students that burned inside them and thus caused them to earnestly seek a greater understanding and appreciation for Him. Well, enough reminiscing, I am sure you all did not call me here for a reunion. I must confess, when I figured out it was the artist Sally Hayes calling me, I just stared at a small sculpture of yours I bought a while ago and my mind drifted away. I do remember something about a recent death and someone having trouble with the grieving process from our chat. Is that why you asked me here?" Jack asked.

"Sort of but first I have to know something. Malcolm if you do not really care for Jack's beliefs, then how did you know his number off of the top of your head?" Sally asked.

"I thought I might be able to use him to shock William into facing the truth. So, when we decided to do this intervention, I memorized his number for a quick reference."

"So, you don't really believe or respect his position. You just want to use him to prove your point?" Sally said with daggers in her eyes.

"I did but . . . . now I think . . . . well he might have something more to offer us." Malcolm conceded.

"Excuse me, I will repeat my question again. Why am I here?" Jack asked rather sternly.

William sat in his chair and smiled, he was not about to tell anything. He had made his peace with the events and it was up to Malcolm to fess up to the truth. Malcolm looked at Sally with a steely gaze to try and make her tell Jack but she refused to look at him. Finally, Malcolm got fed up with the silence.

"You are here because William's wife is still with us . . . . we think." Malcolm said.

"I am not following you. How can his wife still be with us if she is dead?" Jack asked.

"Oh come on! You are a psychic investigator, a ghost buster, you can use some trinket to get the ghost to leave." Malcolm said.

"Wait. You folks think I am a parapsychologist?" Jack asked holding both of his hands up in a stopping manner as he spoke.

"Well, yes. That is what you were into in college and went on through and got your PHD in was it not?" Malcolm asked.

"I was a student of Parapsychology for a time and I did get my undergrad degree in Psychology but my PHDs are in Divinity and Counseling. I specialize in helping people with grief issues. I do not catch ghosts." Jack explained.

It seemed the air of hope had been let out of the room. The sense of hope for clarity in the situation diminished rapidly as Sally and Malcolm felt that they still would not get any better understanding. William noticed the despair on their faces and felt he should at least see if Jack could offer an opinion on any of the events.

"Jack wasn't there a big story in the paper about you investigating a cemetery a while back?" William asked.

"Yes, a local church was building an addition to their Sunday school and, in process of laying the plumbing, they uncovered a body. It turns out to be the very old grave of a fallen soldier from a few centuries ago." Jack said.

"That hardly sounds news worthy. More of an interest piece than a big article." Sally said.

"The body was from the Colonial Period and it showed almost no sign of decomposition."

"A 300 year old corpse should be at least bones, if not dust." William said.

"Well, they opened a few more graves in the cemetery a few yards away and found more fully fleshed corpses."

"A miracle?" William asked in a sheepish manner.

"That is what the local people thought and called me out to investigate. Do not get too excited. It took me a while but I found the answer to the mystery in the trees that surrounded the area. It turns out that back in the Colonial Period, a grove of fruit trees were planted all through the area. These orchards were not properly cultivated and began to cross pollinate with other fruit bearing trees growing wild in the surrounding land. The area was eventually settled and some of the trees were cut down for wood to build the church and others were left alone. Now, there were a few people in the local community that were interred on the church grounds and forgotten by later generations. The fruits matured and fell to the ground. With no one to harvest them they rotted and got absorbed into the soil. People were buried in the soil later and it was assumed that nature had taken its course, until that day. The fruits acted as a natural preservative and extremely slowed the decomposition process. Sorry, no miracle just preserves."

William, Sally and Malcolm had been on the edge of their seats respectively listening to Jack's tale. All of the hope that had left them had now returned and they smiled at each other and nodded in unison that it was time they share their mystery with this open-minded gentleman.

"Jack, we seemed to have a 'miracle' of our own that we need you to investigate." Sally said.

(IN THE STUDIO)

Sally had spent the last hour explaining the events of the past few days and how all of their hunches, theories and ideas had been proven wrong. They had nearly driven themselves mad trying to figure out just what was happening but they did know that this painting was being completed. They just could not figure out by whom. Jack listened to all of the evidence they had gathered intently. He made his right hand into a fist and put it up to his chin as he examined the painting in question. He looked the work of art over and over again and then looked about the room. Finally, after a few minutes, he stopped in his tracks and rubbed his forehead. Malcolm had had enough waiting and wanted an answer.

"So, what do you think, Jack?"

Jack walked back toward them, took a deep breath and let it out as he walked. He stopped at the painting and stared another minute at it. He put his right hand on the painting and tapped his fingers on the top of it as he thought in silence.

"Let me get the facts straight." Jack said as he paced about trying to organize his thoughts.

"You noticed this painting after Rose's death?" Jack asked William.

"Yes, I did not come in here. I felt that this was her 'study' space and that she deserved some privacy. After her death, I just wanted to be near her and this was the best place I could think of to do that. At any rate, art was not one of my favorite pastimes. I respected her chosen profession but I thought it was a little . . . . odd. I know that sounds terrible."

"Actually, it sounds about par for the course." Jack said and shocked everyone in the room.

"The woman he loved put her heart and soul into her art. How can you say such a thing?" Sally scolded.

"I did not say what he said was right or good. William is a scientist. He deals in facts and figures. Only what he can prove with physical evidence. Rose was an artist, someone who casts off conventional thinking and works with her imagination and creativity more so than facts and figures. It is just the nature of your respective fields." Jack explained.

"Okay, but what does that mean for our situation here?" Malcolm asked.

"I am not certain yet but I may have a plan to find out what is going on here." Jack whipped out his cell phone and punched in a few numbers. He walked away from the group and spoke for a few moments and then walked back up to them finishing his conversation. " . . . . and with all that canceled, I will see you on Monday. Bye now." He said and put his phone away.

"What was all of that about?" William asked.

"Oh, I just had to cancel my schedule for tomorrow. It is a Friday, I am sure my students can do without class for one day. Besides we have a mystery here and I plan on figuring out just how it works. So, where can I bunk for the night?"

(IN THE SECOND GUESTROOM)

"Okay, this is their last guestroom. I am staying in the Blue Room and Malcolm is in the Green Room, just next door. I believe they call the one you are in the Yellow or Gold bedroom." Sally said as she ushered Jack into the room.

Jack gave the room a quick look, noticing the golden satin sheets on the bed, the gold colored drapes and gold plated dishes and nightstand. He could tell that the room was not used very much due to the amount of dust on the dresser. He wondered why this room was the second guestroom and not the first but it passed quickly out of his mind. Then he finally responded to Sally.

"Yes, gold indeed. Tell me, if this is their 'backup' guest room, how is their main guestroom decorated?"

"Well, it is similar to this one but is more ornate."

"More ornate than this? Can you elaborate on that statement please?"

"Um . . . the room in painted a light blue, perhaps a sky blue and it even has clouds painted on the wall. It gives me a sense of floating in the clouds and I sleep very well in there. Other than that, it is really not that more special than this room."

"Interesting." Jack said as he rubbed his chin as he thought.

"If you like, I can show it to you now and you can make your own conclusions."

"No, that won't be necessary. However I would like to talk with you more about this situation. If you have the time?"

"Of course but I do not know what else I can tell you that might help you." Sally said as she sat in a chair near the door and made herself comfortable.

"I am not interested about the happenings right now but I am more concerned about your relationship to William and Rose." Jack said as he sat on the edge of the bed.

"Well, what are you asking me?" Sally asked turning her head to the side and giving Jack a very confused and somewhat nasty look.

"I am not under the impression that there was something carnal between any of you here but what I am trying to ascertain is which one of you had the strongest emotional relationship with Rose."

Sally relaxed her gaze as she realized Jack was not suggesting something improper. She reclined in the chair and rubbed her throat as if she were trying to urge the words forward from her memory.

"I suppose that honor would belong to William. He was her husband after all and he must have had the closest relationship to her."

"Don't be too sure. Do not underestimate a girl's relationship to her 'bff' as my students would say. Besides that, you knew Rose before William and Malcolm, right?"

"Yes, she and I were in the Freshmen Dorm together. We were roommates." Sally said as she mulled over her own memories with Jack's questions.

"Ah yes. Roommates were you? That would mean you two were more than friends, you would have formed a familial bond and become sisters."

"I suppose, she was my mother one time." Sally said with a chuckle.

"What does that mean, exactly?" Jack asked as he turned his head to the side in a confused manner.

"There was a time when I needed my Mom's signature on a document and I could not reach her because she was in Europe on one of her 'trips'. I was not going to be able to stay in college without her signature. Rose looked at my Mom's and my handwriting and advised me that our signatures were very close and that I could forge hers. So, I tried and failed miserably. I just was not that kind of artist but Rose was and she studied my Mom's autograph and made a perfect copy. I got to stay in school and we were even better friends."

"Her death hurt you badly as well." Jack insisted.

"Yes, we were close like sisters, as you said and it did hurt me terribly when she passed. I still have trouble believing she is gone but I know she is and I hope she has gone to a better place but I am not sure if I even believe in that spiritual . . . . stuff."

"Really? That is most fascinating. I would expect that from the other two because they are basically scientists, people who are rooted in the physical world. However you and Rose are both artists, people who are not restricted to simple sight and sound. You see things that are not there and make them appear through your art work. You now find yourself asking me for my expertise on matters of a supernatural nature and you say 'you don't believe in the spiritual stuff'?"

"Well . . . I . . . . it   isn't . . . I   mean I   just . . . " Sally stammered on for a moment in a confused stupor. Jack's deductions had made her even more confused about the whole situation. She finally cleared her head and managed to put a sentence together.

"Okay. Let's say you're right about everything. What are you getting at with these questions?"

"I can't tell you just yet. I simply do not have all of the pieces but rest assured I will get to the bottom of this mystery."

(IN THE KITCHEN)

Jack excused himself from Sally's company and made his way to the kitchen for some tea. When he arrived in the kitchen, he noticed that he was not alone. There stood Malcolm pouring himself another cup of coffee. Jack remembered that he had seen Malcolm sipping a cup when he was in the den and that every time he had seen Malcolm, he had seen Malcolm with a cup of coffee.

"Malcolm, just how many cups of coffee does that make for you?"

"What, the authority on 'spirits' has now become an authority on spirited drinks as well? You may believe in a god but that does not make you Him." Malcolm said sorely.

"Malcolm, I know that you and I had our differences in college but I do hope you have put all of that aside. I also hope that you take this whole process seriously."

Malcolm shoved the coffee pot back into the maker violently. He turned to face Jack and summoned all of his anger to his eyes as he stared at Jack and spoke.

"I DON'T CARE ABOUT THIS PROCESS! This is all a joke! I told Sally to call you because I had studied your work and figured that you would show up and destroy this ghost notion that my brother has and he would return to being his regular self but you have just stoked his belief! Now, I have to get rid of you and undo all of the damage that you have caused and now I will probably have to commit my brother after this fiasco."

Jack stirred some honey into his tea and sipped it calmly all through Malcolm's tirade. Jack had seen that type of rage before in the eyes of the people whose miracle he crushed with his findings. He had never meant to deter people from their faith but he felt as though he had but now the rage was not because someone's faith had been crushed but because someone's faith was possibly being confirmed. Jack could see Malcolm's concern for his brother William but knew that Malcolm had buried his concern in his ego.

"'I, I, I, I, I' do you know any other vowels? You are not as concerned with William as you are concerned with how all of this will make you look. Putting William in an institution or retreat or spa or whatever the politically correct term is these days will not help him one bit but it will make you look like a hero and it will allow you to save face within your professional community. I am sure that William's public outbursts made you feel powerless in front of everyone."

Malcolm's rage had lessened as he listened to Jack. He still wanted to punch Jack because he had hit a nerve, a nerve that had needed to be hit. Also, he thought that all of the caffeine he had consumed had helped his rage along. Malcolm took a big gulp to compose himself and then thought carefully about what he wanted to say. He summed up the courage and began his response.

"You are right. As much as I hate to admit it, you are right. I am more concerned about how all of this will reflect back on me. After all, reputation is everything in the professional world."

Jack put his cup down and moved toward the embattled therapist.

"Listen, I am not here to find a ghost. I am here to help your brother grieve and so what if he has to mourn by going on a ghost hunt. Is it really that bad?"

"I suppose not." Malcolm muttered.

"I am sure you have encountered various types of grieving processes in your practice and I would not doubt that they were very destructive?"

"Yes, they were and they usually were self medicated on whatever they could get. No matter what they had to do to get their meds. Which caused even more problems for them and their families."

"And yet William has not resorted to any drugs and he has no history of mental illness or tumors, does he?"

"No, none of that in our family."

"And he did not spend time in Rose's studio inhaling the fumes nor did he work with any tumor causing chemicals, did he?"

"No, but where does that leave us?"

"With Sherlock Holmes." Jack said with a sly grin.

"What?!" Malcolm said in a confused manner.

"If you eliminate the impossible whatever is left no matter how improbable, must be the truth. A famous Holmes's quote. Allow me to explain, William has had no contact with chemicals that could have caused a tumor and he has no history of mental illness, thus the mystery is not a medical one. William is experiencing some type of phenomenon but I have not yet figured it out. However I do believe we might have some answers very soon."

"How do you know?"

"I can't say yet but what I will tell you is that William needs your undivided and nonjudgmental support."

Malcolm took a deep breath and let it out. He looked at the mess he had made with the coffee pot and began to clean it up as he spoke.

"Very well, I will accept your recommendation but I cannot accept that the ghost of my sister in-law is haunting this house."

"Okay, you can have your opinion but please for the love of your brother keep it to yourself as best as you can."

"Fine." Malcolm relented reluctantly.

"Thank you and your brother will thank you." Jack said as he left Malcolm to clean up his mess. Jack headed toward the den to see if he could find William.

(THE DEN)

Jack walked into the den and noticed William staring blankly at the television screen. William had several screens playing but Jack could tell he was not watching any of them. He sat down on the sofa next to William and sipped his tea.

"William, what are you watching?"

"Jericho marathon. I recorded it and have four episodes playing at once."

Jack was confused as to how William could follow the complex plots all at the same time but did not really want an explanation because it would probably be one or two words long and he would not really gain much enlightenment.

"Is this season one or two?" Jack asked.

William shook his head back forth and turned the television off abruptly. He then turned to Jack and gave him a quick glance before he stood up to speak.

"I don't know and don't really care anymore. The show reminds me of Rose."

"How does a series about a nuclear devastated America remind you of your wife?" Jack asked cautiously.

William started to walk away but stopped to explain his statement. He took a deep breath and began his defense.

"Nothing that happened in the series reminds me of her but what happened to the series does. You see, the show was canceled at the height of its popularity and it took a massive campaign to get it back on for just one more season."

"I am afraid I do not follow." Jack said.

"Rose has been "canceled" and I guess this is my campaign to get her back."

"How exactly are you going to get her back?"

"I don't know but I do know what I am feeling. I feel like she is still here and when I sleep I see her and I can hold her again. I just want to stay asleep and be with her." William said as he fought back a tear.

Jack rose to his feet and put his hand on William's shoulder but before he could speak Malcolm offered his own opinion.

"You just want to stay 'asleep' and be with her?! Do you know what you are saying?"

"Malcolm, please remember what we just spoke about." Jack cautioned.

"I don't care! William just alluded to suicide! I cannot support that notion!" Malcolm shouted.

"Bring on the men in white suits and put me in a rubber room then!" William shot back.

"Enough! Both of you sit down, now!" Jack ordered.

Malcolm and William both started to protest but Jack would have none of it.

"I did not say talk! I said SIT!" Jack shouted insistently as he pointed at the nearest sofa.

Both men found a spot to sit and stared up awaiting Jack's next instruction. Sally had heard all of the shouting and rushed into the room wondering what had transpired.

"Sally, there you are. Please, come and join William, Malcolm and I. I need to speak with you all about my findings so far and what I plan to do to solidify my opinion."

"Okay . . ." Sally muttered as she cautiously approached the couch to sit. She smoothed out her dress as she carefully sat, preparing herself for the next outburst.

"Now, William would you be so kind as to get the case from my room that is marked as 'University Property'."

William left the area and in a moment returned with the case in hand. Jack's eyes lit up with excitement as he took the case and carefully opened it on the coffee table.

"What is that? Your ray gun?" Malcolm asked sarcastically.

"No, I keep that in an entirely different case." Jack said without missing a beat.

"So, what is this plan of yours?" William asked.

Jack did not answer but tinkered about in the case. Just as William was about to ask his question again, Jack emerged up from behind the case holding a small video camera.

"My plan is to install these cameras in the studio. I have four here that will cover the corners of the room. William, do you happen to have a video camera here?"

"Yes, I do."

"Please, get it and join us in the studio."

Jack closed the case and thrust it into Malcolm's arms as they walked down the hallway. Jack did not speak during the walk but just tinkered with the camera as he moved the group to the next location. Jack opened the door with his free hand and ushered everyone, including William with camera in hand, into the studio.

"Now, that we are all here, I will tell you the rest of my plan. As I said before, the cameras will be in the corners of the room and what is intended with them is to catch any movement on camera." Jack explained.

"What about my camera? How are you going to use it?" William asked.

"Your camera will be positioned here." Jack said as he stood directly behind the painting facing the image on the canvas.

"Why there?"

"It is simple really. With the four other cameras, we will cover the entire room, monitoring large changes that may happen to the room. With your camera we will focus it on the painting itself. This way we will be able to monitor the most infinitesimal changes to the painting. All of the footage will be recorded to each camera and then it will be sent to the main console that is set up in the den. Each camera can be displayed on the massive television screen in the den area.

"Why record this room only? I have seen Rose in my study and in my bedroom. Why not set up cameras there?"

"The focal point of this whole problem is this painting. While some events have happened in other places, the painting is the only object that actually has changed."

"Wait a minute! How do you know this plan will work? How do you even know if 'Rose' will show up? And what happens if you do catch 'something' floating in the air? What does that prove?" Malcolm shouted in frustration with the whole plan.

William and Sally were unsure of what the plan would accomplish but were willing to try and see if it worked. They were also tired of Malcolm's skepticism by this point. Jack was used to being the skeptic but now he had to defend a claim. He just cleared his throat and responded calmly before the other two.

"The first thing we have to is prove that something IS happening. Once we have proof, we can move forward with a solution. I do not expect you to understand my methods but I would appreciate your quiet respect for the application of the theory."

"I can't! This is ludicrous! Okay, I have had enough! I love you William and when you really want to get help, I will be right there beside you but I cannot listen to this nonsense any longer! Rose is dead! She is gone! I know it hurts to hear that but it is something that you ALL need to understand and come to terms with but not in this way. It is late and I am going to bed." Malcolm said and stormed out of the room.

Sally started to go after Malcolm but William stopped her. He stared her in the eyes and with that look, reassured her that everything would be okay.

"Maybe Malcolm is right." Jack said.

"WHAT?!" Sally said in a shocked manner.

"I mean about the lateness of the hour and getting some sleep. Look, the cameras are all set up and nothing else need be done now.

Let us all just try to relax for the evening." Jack said with the soothing touch in his voice that all good counselors possess.

"I suppose so." Sally said and left the room.

"Good night everybody." Jack said and turned off the light in the studio as William and he walked to their rooms.

"Jack, if we turned the lights off how will the cameras pick up anything?"

"Oh come now, I know you are a man of science with emphasis in Zoology. I was told the animals you care for are wolves and wolves are primarily nocturnal. Surely you have used cameras with 'night vision' capabilities to study them in the wild at some point."

"Yes, I have but my personal camera does not have that setting."

"It is a small matter. You camera is so close to its target it should not matter but just to be on the safe side, why not leave the hall light on tonight."

"Very well." William said as he bid Jack goodnight and made his way to the master bedroom. William closed the door to his room and stared at his bed. It looked so lonely. He cast the thought away by reminding himself there were three other people in the house with him. He did not bother with any of the usual nightly rituals, he just collapsed on the bed. He did not know if he would see Rose tonight or not but he sure was hopeful of the opportunity, even if it were just a dream.

(EARLY IN THE MORNING)

William tossed and turned and finally woke himself up before he tumbled out of the bed and onto the floor. He rubbed his head and face and staggered into the bathroom. He started the faucet and let it run for a few seconds. Then he reached with his right hand to cup the water but just as his hand made it to the falling water, he noticed a dark fluid covering his palm. He pulled his hand close to his face to focus on the odd liquid. He tried to smell it but no aroma could be detected and he was not about to taste it. So, he thrust his hands under the rushing stream and watched the water carry the dark color down the drain.

William grabbed a towel to dry off his hands as he started walking back to his bed. He could not figure out where the oddity had come from and really did not want to think about the possibilities. He wiped his face with the towel as he approached his bed and just as he pulled the towel away, he saw Rose standing before him in the room.

"Rose! Why are you here? You should be in your studio finishing the painting."

Rose put her arms around her husband and engulfed him in a tight embrace. Then she pulled back and looked him in the eyes.

"Tonight, I am here to tell you that I am here and I am with you."

"My love, I have never truly felt that you have left me. I felt so guilty that I was so cold trying to hide my feelings though."

"I am here. I am with you." She said again.

"I know that. It is the people with me who are unsure."

"I am here. I am with you."

William noticed that Rose seemed to grow dimmer. So, he rubbed his eyes to bring her into focus again but when he pulled his hands from his eyes, she was gone. He was not sure what the message meant, so he collapsed back on his bed in hopes of 'reconnecting' with her but just as he got comfortable, he heard a loud feminine shriek coming from the hallway to the studio. He lunged up from the bed like a minuteman ready to fight a redcoat and threw open the door to see if it was Rose calling him to come to her.

William looked to his left to see Malcolm and Jack down the corridor, racing to the scream as well. They arrived to find Sally holding her left hand up to her mouth and pointing at something in the hallway with her trembling right hand. She was petrified with fear, her voice was now silent as she could not even speak and all she could do was point and quiver. William got to her first.

"What is it Sally?!"

Sally could not speak but she did take her eyes off of the object and gave William a glance of utter terror. William finally took a look at the object of her torment and lost his breath for a moment. Then Malcolm and Jack both arrived and took their cues from the other two. They all now stared processing fright and bewilderment at the same time. It was Jack who recovered first.

"I have to check the cameras!" He said and charged to the computer setup in the den.

Malcolm watched as Jack sped past him but he did not take his eyes off of what was before him. He, William and Sally were all highly educated people but now they were staring at something that made them feel as if they were babes in the woods. The hallway had become a place where it seemed that all knowledge ceased as they knew it because they now could literally read the writing on the wall. All of the emotions that washed over them were because of two phrases, written in what appeared to be blood, on the wall.

"I am here. I am with you."

William moved toward the wall as Malcolm and Sally uttered their protests but William could not be stopped. The fear that had gripped him was now replaced with a reassured feeling of love.He remembered that these were Rose's words to him and he knew that Rose would not hurt him or anyone else for that matter. He also knew that from time to time she used a color like the one on the wall. William reached out and touched the large red letter 'I' and then smelt his finger where the liquid had been transferred. Malcolm watched in horror as his brother was not only touching the blood but smelling it as well.

"William, stop that! You don't know where that stuff has been! You could get a disease!"

"From paint?" William said as he turned to face Sally and Malcolm.

"What do you mean?"

"I 'mean' that this is not blood but paint. I remembered that Rose used to paint with this color if she really wanted to evoke a raw emotion in the viewer."

"Well, I would say she got it!" Malcolm exclaimed.

"Are you saying you believe me now?" William asked.

"I don't know about that but I do know what my own two eyes tell me and I know I did not write those words. Did you?" Malcolm asked William.

"No, I did see Rose last night and she told me these very words but I did not leave my bedroom until just a few minutes ago."

"If you didn't write it and I didn't write it and I know Jack didn't leave his room because I would have heard his door shut. So, who could have done it?"

There was a brief moment of silence as the two brothers realized that Sally never offered any proclamation of innocence. They both turned slowly and faced her in order to give her the opportunity to offer her an explanation. Sally knew exactly what the men wanted and she took a big gulp to swallow the lump in her throat. She did not know how to explain but she knew that she would have to tell them something and in a situation like the one they all were in, the truth offers the best answer.

"I do not know what to say, guys. I did not write that on the wall but I know that hand writing . . . "

" . . . . is yours!" Malcolm interrupted.

"Yes, it is in my hand but I promise you that I did not write it!" Sally pled.

"It is okay, Sally. Now you are getting a little taste of what I have been going through for the last few weeks." William said as he comforted her with a hug.

"There is something else." Sally said as she pulled away from William and moved closer to the writing on the wall. "William, did I hear you say that Rose told you these exact words last night in your bedroom?"

"Yes, she did. Why do you ask?"

Sally looked at the ground and then looked at the words again. She knew what she was about to say would sound insane but insanity seemed to be contagious here.

"She told me the same thing last night in my dream, except we were in the studio."

"Has this happened before and you just kept it from me?" William said with a hint of anger in his voice.

"No, I promise you. I was shocked last night in my dream but it felt so real. I guess it is just bizarre."

"You have no idea how bizarre, my dear." Malcolm said. He had been quiet while Sally and William began conversing but now he found a place to enter the conversation. Sally and William had almost forgotten he was there because they were so consumed with their discussion. Now they were well aware of his presence and felt an odd aura in the air that Malcolm was about to have a revelation of his own.

"What exactly are you talking about, Malcolm?" William asked.

"Shared dreams just do not happen. It is possible that people can have like or similar dreams especially if they are in the same situation but for three people to have the same dream about a certain person uttering the exact same statement goes well beyond the borders of 'the unheard of'." Malcolm explained.

"So, what DO you believe?" William asserted.

"'I don't know but I would guess . . . . ' "

" . . . . THE PAINTING!" William shouted interrupting his brother's continued explanation and raced down the passageway toward the studio.

William pushed open the door and went straight to the canvas. Malcolm and Sally got there right when William began examining the painting. They looked at each other apprehensively as they waited to hear what William had found. Was the painting complete? Was this odd 'dream' over? Would life now go back to normal? They noticed the look on William's face changed from a hopeful excitement to one of confusing disappointment, like a child would have on Christmas if they did not get the toy they wanted.

"William what do you see?!" Sally asked.

"Nothing." William said in a defeated manner as he sank into the chair to stare at his wife's unfinished work of art.

"Nothing?! Is the canvas blank now?" Malcolm asked.

"No, it is still the same but there is no change to it and I just thought that it might be complete."

"But we all had the same dream?" Sally said offering up the question to anyone but not really expecting an answer.

"We did? WE DID!" William said loudly as he stood up from the chair and moved toward the others.

"What is it now, William?" Sally asked.

"WE . . . . did have the same dream! Didn't you hear what he said back in the hallway?" William said as he pointed at Malcolm.

William could tell Sally was trying to remember but her memory was still a bit shot from all that had happened.

"Sally, we were standing next to the wall and he offered up an explanation about shared dreams and their impossibility. Then he went on to talk about how similar dreams were possible."

"Yes, I do remember that."

"Then he said something to the effect that for THREE people to have the same dream, about the same person, saying the same sentence was unheard of."

"Three people?" Sally said trying to confirm what she had heard.

Malcolm knew that his slip had been discovered and he also knew that he would now have to explain what he had experienced. He wanted to try and bury his response in Psychological vagueness but knew that William would tear right through his stalling tactic. Malcolm cleared his throat and fidgeted where he stood for a moment and finally gave up on trying to spin what had happened.

"Okay, Okay . . . I admit it. I too had a dream about Rose last night and in it we were in William's Study. Rose just kept saying those two statements over and over."

"Malcolm, welcome to the crisis brother. It is good to have you." William said with a big smile and hugged his brother. Malcolm pushed him away because he this was not an experience that he wanted to share with his brother.

"Whatever you say but I am still not convinced. By the way, where has Jack gotten off to?"

They began to retrace their steps back to the wall, hoping to find the answer that they sought coming back to their memory. Just as they all reached the wall and took a quick glance at the dark red writing. They heard a shout of frustration emanating from the den area

(THE DEN)

William, Malcolm and Sally approached the den slowly because they were unsure of what exactly they might find. Malcolm and Sally remembered how upset William was at the beginning of this journey and they feared that the most objective person in their little group may have just had an unsettling break in composure. William knew that nothing bad could have happened because Rose was not an aggressive person but he was unsure of what could have made such a poised man get so rattled.

"Jack, is everything okay?" William asked leading the group into the room.

"Yes, everything is normal. That is the problem!" Jack said as he stood close to the screen of the large television watching every picture in picture that had been recorded the previous night.

"What exactly do you mean?"

"I thought that with the happening, (He motioned his hand in the direction of the hallway as he spoke.) there might actually have been some activity caught on camera."

"I'm sorry, Jack. We just checked the painting and it is the same as it was last night." William consoled.

"So, apparently the only activity was that message to Malcolm."

The room got extremely quite with Jack's assertion. Up until now, every activity had been solely focused on William and now it seemed that Rose had taken an interest in Malcolm. They were all confused but none more so than Malcolm.

"Why me?!" Malcolm asked slowly rising from the chair that he had plopped down in when he entered the room.

"Perhaps it is your constant skepticism. Your refusal to accept what your eyes are telling you? I cannot say for certain but I do remember your rant last night. You said, and I quote, 'Rose is gone. Rose is not here.' And I believe she has answered you, a hundred fold, it seems that she might not be too happy with you." Jack explained.

Malcolm sat down on the sofa to wrap his mind around the fact that the spirit of his dead sister-in-law was now trying to quarrel with him from beyond the grave. He rubbed his face with his hands and Sally sat down beside him to comfort his troubled nerves. William stood and gazed at the screens, then looked down the hallway and came to a conclusion.

"I think you are wrong, Jack." William said.

Time seemed to stop because for the first time it was William, the believer, with an assertion that seemed to go against one of Jack's theories.

"How so?" Jack asked.

"Rose told us all this same message but she did not say as a warning or a threat. It was more of an assurance. It was as if she were trying to put us all at ease with this whole experience."

"Are you really sure it was her message?"

"Of course, why would you ask that question?" William asked with a little vinegar in his voice because of Jack's disbelief.

"I do not mean to upset you but I heard your conversation in the hall about the hand writing. Perhaps it was Sally's and now we have discovered the sweet and elaborate plan of hers to help you let Rose go?"

Malcolm ceased his worrying and scooted away from Sally on the couch as everyone turned to look at her. Sally, at first, had a look of shock on her face but then took a breath and got up from the couch before she spoke. Everyone was on the edge of their seat at the possibilities that Sally could enlighten. Had she really been the architect for this whole scam? How did she fool all of the PhDs in the room for so long? What would they do now that Sally was going to confess and how would this confession affect their friendship?

"Yes, that writing on the wall is in my hand but I PROMISE I DID NOT WRITE IT! Rose was my best friend in the entire world and I miss her terribly but I would never put William, her truest of loves, through any torment at all especially of this sort because I know Rose would never forgive me. Now, I have explained that I was not in the country for some of these events and that I never conspired with anyone! If you all (She waved her and shook it at each man as she spoke.) want to blame someone and I am your best culprit, I suggest you men turn in your PHD's because they are not worth the paper on which they are printed!"

Sally began to storm out of the room but William stopped her.

"Listen to me, everyone! I know this is Rose and I know it is not a plan of any sort. I can feel her still in this house, even now. I cannot go to a room and find her. I have tried to look for her but I cannot find her but I still feel her. She is here. You all are just now understanding my position. You can see why I have been 'off my game' but I have come to terms with it. I believe now and once I gave myself to this belief, I felt convicted of it and that conviction has given me a renewed sense of peace. I know that this may sound crazy to you but once you open your heart and mind up to it, the possibilities become endless. I see worry and concern on all of your faces but look at me. I am not worried and I am not concerned anymore. You guys just have to believe."

A new silence engulfed the room. No one really knew what to say or at least what they wanted to say. William had just had a major breakthrough it seemed but Sally and Malcolm were not sure if William's insanity had actually infected them or if he had gone so insane that he had actually made an entire loop on the crazy train and come back to sanity again. Jack on the other hand had been nodding his head back and forth all through William's speech. He walked toward William and just as he got to him, he turned away to speak to Sally.

"I owe you an apology, my dear."

"What for?" Sally asked as if she were coming out of some type of mental fog.

"I went into instructor mode for a moment back there when I accused you. Usually, I will do that to one of my seniors when they make a bold assertion in class and then I force them to defend their beliefs. Most of the time, they will defend their point like a Spartan in a phalanx but when I questioned you, I seemed to have caused an uproar. I never meant for that to happen, even though you defended yourself quite well. I believe my students would say, 'we got served'."

"Well, I did not mean to be so blunt but I felt like I had to be."

"Of course you did and might I ask a question?"

"Sure." Sally said uncertain of what his query might be.

"When we spoke a while ago, you told me an interesting story about how Rose helped you stay in college."

"Yes . . . . she forged my Mom's handwriting so that I could stay in college. Why does that matter?"

"Actually, it matters a great deal. If Rose could forge someone's signature in college, perhaps she kept up the talent over the years, practicing it and now using it from beyond the grave."

"Why though? If she could . . . . Why did she . . . . " Sally stammered and Jack answered before she could get her thoughts formed into a question.

"I believe I heard William speak of how Rose liked to use that deep red color when she wanted to evoke profound emotions on people and I think he is right. The message and color drew all of us in and we put aside any doubts we had for the moment and really began wrapping our minds around the concept of her still being . . . . among us. I think that last night's event was a message not to just Malcolm. I think Rose used every tool possible to send all of you a message."

"And if she wrote a message from her to Malcolm, in my handwriting, I would have to accept that it was her doing it and not a hoax. I would have to rely on faith and see what cannot be seen. Rose was always into the spiritual side of things. Life has a purpose and all of that. There is a great plan at work type stuff. But then why would she appear to each of us?" Sally questioned.

"I can only guess that if she had not appeared in each of your dreams last night, that when you all awoke this morning and saw the message, you probably would not have wanted the help of a Seminary Professor, in short a Preacher, but you probably would have kicked me out and have run to the nearest psychic or have taken the scholarly professional route and either gone into deep therapeutic analysis or just packed up and ran away from this house all together and pretended that the whole occurrence did not happen." Jack said and then turned back to continue to analyze the screens on the television.

"He's not wrong. I am ashamed to say." Malcolm said.

"Yes, I probably would have consulted a mystic of some sort." Sally added.

"Wait a second! You are holding something back. Aren't you?" William asked Jack and garnered everyone's attention.

Jack continued to look at the screens but let out a sigh and made a big grin. He paused the action on the screens and turned and faced William.

"Yes, but I just did not want to alarm you further."

"Alarm us further!" William shouted.

"What did you find? Something on the tape? Are waiting for one us to start bawling before you show us?" Malcolm asked.

"Please, tell us everything." Sally pleaded.

"Well, I was waiting because you all have had a pretty good brush with faith this morning and I wanted to help you down this road slowly because I do not know if you all can handle this much faith this soon." Jack stated.

"Just tell us!" William asserted.

"Fine, the dreams last night, the writing on the wall, even the forging of a certain person's handwriting are all signs of cognition. Someone or something thought this out and put it into motion."

"So, are you going against your previous belief in the 'occurrence' and are now saying that a person IS responsible?" William asked.

"I think Rose's spirit is responsible but we really have no proof to show for it."

"Are you mad? Look at that wall! You just laid out all of the evidence and now you saying we have no evidence?" Sally shouted.

"All of those events together, prove that Rose is here and has been, for some time, working on that painting and conversing with William but we have no tangible evidence to prove our beliefs to the outside world. The wall could be explained as if you are lying because you are an artist and it is not hard to imagine that you could forge someone's writing and the dreams could be explained as anything from Post Traumatic Stress to alcohol. This is why I am upset that our cameras did not catch anything because we have only our eyewitness testimonies and for this type of event, even our prestigious reputations as scholars and professionals would not help. In fact we might actually do more damage to our reputations if we came forward with what evidence we have collected."

A blanket of silence and frustration fell over the room. They all had felt something scary but real for the first time and wanted to share what had happened to them all but with Jack's explanation, their hopes were dashed. They had gone from skeptics to believers in a very short time and were unsure of their next step. William had believed for a bit longer but had had no way of telling Sally or Malcolm how he had come to his conclusions. Now, they were in the same place as he had been, scared and confused. However, he had made his peace with what was happening and was now more excited than afraid. He could believe openly about Rose and now his family would believe him, he felt, but first he knew he had to bring their morale up.

"Jack, I see your point about going public but I do not believe that Rose wanted us to do that, at least not yet anyway."

"Interesting theory. Can you elaborate?" Jack asked.

"First, I am not one of your students. Second, the painting is why she is still here. She has to finish it before she can rest or go to Heaven. Last night's activity was to get us all in the same frame of mind or at least to get us to believe in something greater than ourselves, a purpose for our lives. At any rate her message is to us and not the world. We just have to relax and let her do the talking and not try too hard to put words or meanings to the events that happen. Just let go and let . . . . God." William said cautiously.

"You believe in God now, William?" Malcolm asked.

"Brother, can you look at what has happened here and tell me, with a straight face, that you don't believe that there is a powerful force that is enabling Rose to do all of this? I know you always hate 'Intelligent Design' discussions but we have seen the proof of intelligence here and I have to believe there is a design to all of it." William said all of this and then turned his attention to the screens where Jack had been staring. The room was silent for just a moment as everyone took in the intense feelings William had just conveyed.

"So, what is our next move?" Sally asked to break the heavy silence that had overwhelmed them.

Everyone looked to Jack. He had been the captain on this voyage down the river of impossibilities, so far and they hoped he could help them get back home, sane.

"I have been thinking about that but I still feel that I am missing something on the videos. Maybe if we each took a camera and watched the footage, we could meet back up later tonight and discuss what we found."

"AUGGH, you are always missing something! So, you are giving us homework?" Malcolm asked frustrated.

"Not exactly, I think that we each have a different set of eyes with a different perspective and if we each took a camera, we might just find the answers we seek. Also, I think it would be a good idea for each of us, when we finish viewing the footage, to keep the cameras on us and filming at all times. Since things seem to happen at any time and in different places in the house, it appears that neither the house nor the painting is the focus but that the people are and if something does happen, one of us should be able to catch it on tape."

"This sounds like the best plan we can get so let's just go with it but what about the fifth camera? Who gets it?" William asked.

"I do not think it will be needed but we will have if we need it. I have already viewed that footage at high speed while you all were milling about a while ago and there is nothing on it. That camera was focused on the painting itself and we all know nothing happened there last night but maybe something happened in the room or on the peripheral. Just take your time and see what you can. We all were up early this morning and we have been going nonstop since that time. We have spent the morning trying to figure out what to do and now we have made it to early afternoon. I say we get something to eat and then we start watching videos. Hopefully we will be able meet back up at around 8pm and have something more to talk about then.

Everyone agreed with Jack's plan and got some snacks from the kitchen. Once the small meal was complete and their bellies were satisfied, they each took a camera and went off to view the footages separately. They knew they each had around eight hours of film to watch and they wanted to keep to the 8pm appointment as best as they could.

(9:05PM)

Everyone had completed their tasks and returned to the den area eager to discuss what they had found or rather what they had hoped each other had found because each of their footage had been different angles of the same room where nothing had happened. Their hopes were high that somebody had seen something. Everyone accept Jack because he was the only one who had not yet made it back to the den. Finally, the anticipation began to mount to the point of eruption in Malcolm and he could not wait any longer.

"Where is Jack?!" He shouted half hoping that Jack would hear the ire in his voice and make a hasty entrance.

"Calm down, I am sure he will be along soon." Sally soothed.

"Well, Jack is over an hour late. Perhaps he fell asleep?" William offered.

"Okay fine. We can go check on him." Malcolm said and started toward Jack's room with Sally and William not far behind.

They passed by the hallway where the words were emblazoned on the wall and then to the bedroom hall and finally made it to Jack's door.

(Bang, Bang, Bang)

Malcolm pounded on the door to awaken Jack if he happened to be sleeping but nothing happened. Malcolm took a deep breath and laid into the door again a little harder this time.

(BANG, BANG, BANG)

But still there was no answer. Malcolm had had enough of the waiting and tried the door knob. To his surprise, the door was not locked. So, he gave a look back to everyone, shrugged his shoulders and entered the room.

"Malcolm, you could at least announce yourself before you go barging into someone's living area!" Sally chided as she grabbed Malcolm by the arm to prevent him from entering the room.

"It is his fault. He should have answered the door."

They began bickering back and forth as William slipped past them and into the room to begin the investigation and it was not long before he found something quite startling. He moved to the desk where Jack appeared to have been working and found a note. He turned around to share the note with the others but still heard them arguing in the hallway.

"Will you two children stop!? We have a situation here." William said as he emerged from the room and held up the note.

"What is that?" Malcolm asked.

"It looks like a note." Sally fired at Malcolm.

"STOP! Both of you! Jack is not in his room!" William shouted as he pointed into the room from the doorway.

"I didn't hear him say that he was leaving? Try his phone." Malcolm said.

Sally punched in the numbers on the card that Malcolm had given her a few days ago. Everything became silent as they waited for Sally to make contact with Jack and find out where he had gone. As they waited, they happened to hear the faint sounds of a ringtone blaring out the chorus of a song saying 'You found me'. William and Malcolm both heard the song and tracked the sound into Malcolm's room and to the desk where William had found the note. They shuffled some papers and books about and finally discovered the phone. William looked at the number displayed on the screen and recognized it as Sally's.

By this time, Sally had followed the ringing too and was standing in the doorway watching as William held up the phone to indicate that she had gotten the right number but that Jack was not going to be answering the phone. Sally closed her cell phone and put it back in her pocket. The three looked at each other in disbelief and then Sally broke the stunned silence.

"What is written on that note?"

"Not much. A bunch of numbers and then by the last number there is the word 'possessions'." William answered.

"Possessions? Oh, I see. He must have forgotten something and went somewhere to get it and bring it back." Malcolm asserted.

"What object could be that important that he would drop everything and leave us without warning?"

"I don't know. He said he was a Preacher, maybe he went to get his Bible or crucifix or some other ghost ridding tool of the church?"

"Now that is just silly! Surely, he would have shared with us what he found before he went out and got something of his?"

"Maybe he didn't leave of his own accord? Maybe he got too close and . . . . something happened?" Malcolm said wiggling his fingers for a childishly spooky effect.

Before William could fuss at Malcolm, Sally interrupted their debate with a fact of her own.

"Boys, his car is not in the driveway. He left in a powerful hurry and went somewhere but where and for what is the question?"

"What possession could he have gone to retrieve and why was it so important?" Malcolm asked in earnest this time. He had been sarcastic with William and Sally recently because he was still struggling with his beliefs but this new turn of events gave him some room to regain some of his skeptic footing. However, with Sally's revelation, he was brought back to the serious side of the situation.

They stood in the hallway trying to decide what their next move should be but before they could put a plan together, there came a knock at the front door. William shoved the note into the front pocket of his pants and they all raced to the front, relieved in the notion that Jack had just been out for a drive and now found himself locked out of the house. William reached the front door first and opened it quickly, ready to welcome Jack back into his home.

However, when William opened the door he did not see Jack standing there but a Police officer instead. This was not just any Police Officer though, it just happened to be the very same officer he had had a run in with the other day in his back yard. The Policeman recognized William too and spoke first.

"It's you again?! I thought this house looked familiar!"

"Officer, why have you come to my house again? I know I was not out on the lawn this time."

"Actually, I am here about an acquaintance of yours. Do you know a Dr. Jack Watson?" The officer said as he read the name from a notepad in his breast pocket.

Malcolm and Sally had been listening a few steps away but when they heard Jack's name mentioned, they hurried up to the door to hear everything the officer had to say.

"I suppose all of you know this gentleman." The cop asserted as he watched Sally and Malcolm push the door open completely and stand there anxiously awaiting what news the man had for them about their new acquaintance.

"Officer, please tell us what has happened." William pled.

"He was involved in 10-50, that's a car wreck, early today. He is at the hospital in recovery. Don't bother going down there because the hospital will tell you that only family are allowed to see him right now. He had some nasty cuts that would require stitches but he was in surgery for the damage done to his leg, when I left to come here. His leg was broken in a few places and they are repairing the damage as we speak. But if you really want to help, what you can do is tell me what was going on here. (The officer waited for their response and they each managed a nod of acceptance) We are still piecing together the details but what we have determined is that he was traveling at high speed and lost control of his vehicle while attempting to negotiate a curve a few miles from here. Witnesses stated that he had driven to the campus, retrieved something and/or someone from an office and was hurrying back in this general direction, I think we can now assume that he was headed here but we still do not know why? What were you all doing here?"

"This is my home and he was helping me . . . . with a problem." William said as he handed his identification over to the officer.

"Wait a minute! You're the therapist brother of his right?" The officer said as he pointed to Malcolm, checked William's information and handed it back.

"Yes, yes I am." Malcolm said as he handed over his driver's license.

"So, was Dr. Watson helping you?"

"He was helping all of us. He is a Professor of Divinity at the local college."

The officer looked at Malcolm's license and gave it back as he nodded his head to what Malcolm had said. The officer looked at each of them one more time and then reached into his pocket and recovered the compact video camera that Jack had been examining. The camera had a small note attached to it. The officer held it in his hands as he spoke.

"The professor was clutching this in his hand at the hospital. I managed to pry it from his hands when, I promised to bring it to you. He said something odd but I told him I would tell you, so I wrote it down on this note so I could get it straight."

The officer looked at the note and read it aloud to them in hopes that they could shed some more light on the meaning of the message.

"'The spirit is with you.' That is all he said before he passed out. I didn't think it made much sense but now that I have been talking with you, I might have a plausible theory, of sorts."

"What do you mean? Please, enlighten me!" Malcolm asked he felt that he had more education and experience than the officer and yet the officer had been able to gain some meaning out of the madness and he could not. He had to know what insight the policeman could possibly offer.

"Well, you said that Dr. Watson is a Professor of Divinity, which makes him a Preacher. When we talked to people at the college, they all said that he specialized in several areas but grief counseling was his main field of study. Now, given what I know about you from our last meeting (he said as he motioned his hand in William's direction), I can venture a guess that he was helping you, along with these other people, to process your wife's death. However, what does not make sense is the gentleman that was with Dr. Watson in the car."

"What? Who was with him in the car?" William asked.

"A Dr. Goldenberg. He is a Professor of Technology at the university. Eye witnesses say that Dr. Watson arrived at the college and rushed into Dr. Goldenberg's office. The two had a closed door meeting for a few minutes and then they both hurried out of the building and into Dr. Watson's car. Some said they saw Dr. Goldenberg carrying a brief case but no one could say what was in it. It appears that they had what they needed and were hurrying back here."

"What did Dr. Goldenberg say about all of this?"

"When he wakes up, we will ask him. He was not wearing his seatbelt and was thrown from the vehicle on the initial impact, thankfully there were a lot of thick bushes and his back absorbed the brunt of the landing. He is still unconscious but the doctors are hopeful that both men will make a full recovery. So, that leaves this camera and Dr. Watson's message as our only clues. I looked at the footage on the camera but I did not see anything except, what looked like security tape, of an art studio. I am not supposed to relinquish this evidence but we made a copy of the tape and I do not think the camera will be of any more use. However, if you find anything, you be sure to call me. Here is my card (The officer said as he handed his contact information to William.) I am heading back to the hospital right now and if I hear anything I will let y'all know about it."

"Thank you officer. We appreciate your consideration." William said.

The officer returned to his car and pulled out of the driveway. William, Sally and Malcolm were all exhausted from watching the tape but they knew they had to see what inspired Jack to race off without telling anyone and get some object and even bring another person into our little secret. They set the camera up to play on the big screen in the den so that they all could watch what happened on the video.

They all had been already been watching an empty room all day and now they found themselves watching the same empty room over the same hours of the same night but from a different point of view. They did their best to remain focused but by the fifth hour some of them were too worn to continue.

"I have had enough. This day has been one LONG emotional rollercoaster and I am going to bed." Malcolm announced.

"But what about the professors and the notes? This video is our best clue yet and you are going to leave before we have a chance to completely examine this evidence?" Sally asked.

"Look, my plan is to get some sleep right now. Maybe tomorrow one of the two professors will be awake and we can just let them tell us what they found. Apparently, it is worth dying for, so they should be eager to share. We have watched thirteen hours of film with no results, correction we have watched thirteen hours of nothing. You two can keep going but I plan to get some sleep. Hey, maybe Rose will come to us again tonight and fill us in then, we can put this whole mess aside and get on with our lives and let her get on with her . . . . whatever."

"Still struggling with belief Malcolm?" William asked sarcastically.

Malcolm just scoffed and walked down the hallway to his room without offering a witty reply to his brother's remark since he was in no mood for a fight. William had stood up to speak and now remained standing as he looked wearily at the uninteresting video. He let his head hang as he thought about another three hours of this and did not really want to watch anymore, at least not at that time. He looked down at Sally and she read the look on his face as if he had written it on his forehead with a Sharpe Marker.

"No, you are not going to bail on me too, are you?" Sally asked.

"For once, I think Malcolm is right. I think if we get some sleep and pick back up with this in the morning. Hopefully we will have better luck. Maybe one of the professors will be awake or at least have moaned something that we might be able to use. At any rate, we will be more rested." William reasoned.

"But what if we have not gotten to the right part yet? If we just watch it a little further, maybe we will see something."

"Sally, what if we have already went past it? We are so tired from the dreams last night, the shocks this morning and this evening. We may have seen it but just missed it. Look, I want to get to the bottom of this mystery as much as you but I doubt we will do it tonight."

"I am going to keep watching. I just think we are too close to give up now." Sally avowed.

"Very well, I applaud your resilience. Please continue with my blessing. If you find something, do not hesitate to wake me up."

"Thank you William and you will be the first to know." She said and then looked down at the coffee table.

William noticed the slight look of disgust on her face and thought that he would have to address it.

"Don't worry about the mess on the coffee table. That is just what my brother and I would do when we wanted to get comfortable and watch TV when we were kids and I guess it is an old habit to break. Rose did not care for it either." William said as he pointed to a couple of piles of manly debris consisting of wallets, change, paper and whatever else they might have had when they sat down and emptied their pockets.

"It's okay. We all have been a little busy lately and also, I am a sculptor, so I understand messy tables and desks. I guess it just surprised me at all of the stuff you guys keep in your pockets at one time. I suppose if you were to dump my pocket book out on the table, it might look just as bad."

William nodded and made his way down the dimly lit hallway to his bedroom. Sally watched him wearily stagger his way down the hall and wondered if he would make it or just lay on the floor in the corridor. Finally, she saw him turn the corner at the end of the hall, then she listened for and heard the close of his bedroom door. She laughed to herself about the whole situation and then put the moment aside because she knew that she still had three more hours of video to scan through. She grabbed up the remote and took a deep breath as she sat down and unpaused the video. It had been a long day and it was shaping up to be a long night.

(1:00 AM)

Sally brushed her hair out of her face as she sat up in the sofa trying to refocus her energy. She felt her zeal for answers giving way to the exhaustion that assailed her body. She rubbed the back of her neck as she stood to stretch and hopefully regain some of her energy but it was a futile attempt. She looked away from the video for just a moment, gazing longingly down the hallway that led to her bedroom. She knew she needed some rest and felt that a 30 minute break might not hurt so she paused the video and made her way down the hall. She saw the welcoming door to her room, opened it and walked into the room. There she found the bed and its magically comfortable covers invitingly lit by the small lamp beside her bed. She climbed into the bed and pulled the covers over her body and wrapped up in a blanket of warmth as she waited for sleep to take her away. Then she rolled over to her left almost asleep and felt someone touch her shoulder. She rolled back over thinking it was William or Malcolm wanting to discuss another dream but when she got the person in full view, she could see that it was Rose standing by her bed.

"The professor's note!" Rose said and vanished as quickly as she had appeared.

Sally snapped back to reality. She looked around and realized that she was still in the den and had fallen asleep on the couch. She looked at her watch and it read 1:00 am but she had lost track of time so she looked outside, it was still dark. The video was still playing and she wondered if she had missed her opportunity. She hung her head and shook it in disgust at herself as a feeling of failure swept over her. Then she remembered the vivid dream she had just had and what Rose had told her.

"'The professor's note?' All that said was some trivial message. How is that important without the professor's explanation?" Sally debated aloud hoping that vocalizing her thoughts might bring clarity to the situation and maybe even a solution.

Then she remembered the other note that William had found in Jack's room. She tried to see what had been written on it but could not picture it in her head. Then she recalled that she had seen William put it in his pocket when they had heard the policeman banging on the door.

Sally looked down at the piles of what appeared to be trash on the coffee table. She could not tell which was Malcolm's and which was William's so she searched the closest one to her. A cloud of debris consisting of wallets, watches and coins and cards fluttered about as Sally forced her way through the pile but found nothing. She moved on to the next pile and scattered the bits of paper about carefully this time and finally found the crumpled up square shaped note the professor had scribbled on earlier. She stared down at the note to try and make sense of it.

"44105
45202
50000 possession"

She read aloud to try and figure out what it meant. She looked up to try and gather her thoughts. Her eyes wandered around the room and she rolled the numbers over and over in her head. Then by chance her eyes found their way to the video screen again. She still did not see anything happening but then something seemed to jump out at her and she could not for the life of her think of a reason that she had not seen it before. There it was in the bottom corner of the screen, she watched as the numbers changed from 341.23 to 341.24 and 341.25.

"It's the time!" She said loudly and then covered her mouth as she looked down the hall hoping that she had not awoken anyone with her outburst. When she was satisfied that everyone was still tucked

safely in their beds, she picked up the remote and fast forwarded the
tape to the correct times.

440.55

440.56

440.57

440.58

440.59

441.00

441.01

441.02

441.03

441.04

441.05

Finally she had made it to the first number. The painstaking
process had finally reached its destination. She paused the film to
stare at the screen to see if she could find what morsel of truth Jack
had uncovered but she did not see anything. Then she resumed the
tape and backed it up a few frames and allowed it to run at a slower
speed. Nothing was seen at first but then it the top corner of the
screen she saw something shadowy move. She could not make it out,
so she paused the tape and enlarged that portion but still could not
bring the image in focus. It was definitely some type of movement
but she could not tell what it was.

Sally looked to the paper at the next number on the note '45202'
and fast forwarded the tape to that time. As she got close to the time,
she allowed the film to play hoping her tired eyes would catch the
movement again. Then just as the time on the screen ticked down to
the time on the note, she saw the movement again and paused it. She
could not believe what she stood there and saw on the screen. In the
same blown up section, she could clearly see an arm. A human arm!
Not a ghostly apparition of an arm but a human arm in full view. It
moved about up and down and then went out of the frame. She let

the video play for a few seconds more just out of curiosity to see if something else could be seen but then gave up and pushed on to the last time on the note.

She got the time close and then allowed the tape to play. She wanted to be certain that she did not go past the time indicated. Finally, Sally put the note up to the screen and watched as the times lined up perfectly. She stared intently at the same position where the activity had been witnessed before and almost could not contain her excitement. The mysterious arm reappeared in view but this time she could see more of it, all the way up to the shoulder and she could see the neck and hair of the man painting but was still unable to decipher which man. Then the man turned his head to the side and she got a complete profile. The profile was all she needed to tell who it was. She dropped the remote and stood in shock as she processed fear and elation. She turned off the screen, unplugged the camera and put it on the coffee table as she sat down and stared blankly at the camera as she tried to organize her thoughts aloud.

"I can't believe it but no one will believe me unless I can prove it beyond a shadow of a doubt and a side profile is not enough. I know why Jack left in such a hurry and was trying to get back so fast. He was getting the proof he needed but I believe I can get it now."

(WILLIAM'S BEDROOM)

William's restlessness continued as he tried to sleep. He adjusted the pillow and then the covers on his bed and finally just rolled over on his left side. Just as he had thought that he had gotten comfortable, he felt the restlessness come over him again but knew he was just too tired to get up so he lay on his side and opened his eyes.

"Hey Rose." He said because when he opened his eyes, she was laying there beside him and facing him in their bed.

"Hello, my love." She said in a warm loving tone with her deep green eyes staring into his light blues.

"You look tired dear." William said as he repositioned himself closer to her on the bed without changing his sideways position.

"Last night took a lot out of me."

"I imagine so. You scared the crap out of everyone but I know what you were trying to tell them and I smoothed it over for you.

"I am sure you did. It is actually the reason for my visit tonight."

"Another message? Perhaps you could just tell me it and I will relay it on to everyone. I am certain they will listen now." William assured.

"I am sure they would but the events of last night and yesterday in general have made me see the depth of trouble I have caused to our family and even beyond them. I never meant to hurt anyone, I just wanted you to have something to remember me by. I had to finish my Magnum Opus. I really wanted us to be a family. Us and our children but I see that I was never meant for that gift, to be a mother. I knew that with my art, I could combine your work and my work and in a sense, together we could make a beautiful family portrait."

"I am not sure I understand but I am willing to believe without knowing, you have taught me that much."

"William, this will probably be the last time you see me."

"What do you mean? You are leaving me?" William said as he sat up in the bed but kept his eyes trained on Rose.

"William, I died a time ago. I cannot stay with you like this anymore." Rose said as she reached up from the bed and stroked his shoulder to comfort him.

"I know you died. I suffered through your funeral and wake and I have been suffering until just recently, when I made my peace with your death."

"I know that was another reason I was allowed this opportunity, to help you."

"Who gave you . . . . ?" William started to ask but Rose stopped him before he could finish his question.

"William, I do not have time to explain and besides I do not think that you are up for that leap of faith, yet. Just trust me and let's make the most of the gift we have now by not wasting it on questions and spend the time we have finishing what we started."

William hung his head and tried to think of a clever come back that would rally Rose to his side and they could spend more time trying to figure out how he could keep her there with him. His mind raced with ideas but they were all scientific and he knew that the situation had progressed well beyond the realm of science. Then he felt Rose's gentle touch on his hand and looked up to see her trying to lead him out of their room. He got out of bed and followed her, still trying to think of a way but then he looked up from his fruitless ideas and noticed how beautiful she looked. She was always an attractive lady but now there was a light about her that made her shine like a full sappy moon glowing over freshly wetted roses making them sparkle as if they had diamonds on them.

"What are you doing?" Rose said and shocked William out of his enjoyment.

"I was just admiring how unbelievably gorgeous you look as you walk down the hallway."

"It doesn't matter if we're alive or dead you men think of one thing." Rose said as she smiled and laughed.

"No, that wasn't what I was talking, about . . . . but is there a possibility that we could . . . "

"Are you just going to stand there and stutter on about nonsense or are you going to be a gentleman and open the door for a lady?" Rose asked interrupting William's thought. He moved forward and opened the door for her but still wanted his question answered.

"Hey, if this is the last time I will see you . . . . " He said with a sly grin on his face.

"William, my dear, there are much bigger obstacles for us to accomplish tonight. We do not need to become focused on a portion of our relationship that does not stand the test of time but what we will do, will be of great importance. Not just for us but for our family." Rose said as she moved close to him and put her index finger up to his lips to silence him.

William watched as she entered the room and walked over to the easel where her last painting waited for her to finish. All he could do was stare. He loved her so much and even though a part of him still clamored for an answer to his question, he knew that she was right. He did not know why she was right but felt that she was and that he had to trust that instinct.

"Are you coming? We have a bit of work to do and not a lot of time to do it." Rose asked as she looked up from the easel and patted her hand in the seat of a chair right beside her.

William looked at her bathed in the only light in the room, a small lamp focused directly on the painting, all of the physical love left him as he watched her get ready to work. His love was now a pure love, an eternal love. The camera that had been there was now removed and that space was where Rose had reserved a chair so that he could help her finish the painting. He looked about the darkened room as he slowly made his way to her. His love for her had never been this great, the peaceful purity of loving someone because of the person they are. This might be the last time he saw her but he wanted to remember every infinitesimal detail.

(EARLIER IN THE DEN)

Sally quietly fumbled with the camera and made sure that what she recorded would also be recorded on the main television to allow her to prove what she thought and saw. Finally, everything checked out to be functioning well, so she moved toward the hall where she believed the activity would take place. Then just before she made it into the corridor, she heard a door in the hall open and footsteps make their way onto the hardwood floor.

Sally ducked down behind the connecting wall and waited quietly for the steps to get further away from her. She heard two distinct voices that seemed to belong to the footsteps. She knew both of the voices but could not bring herself to accept the second voice she heard. She stared down at the camera and began to curse her fate.

"Why did this happen to me? I am not the preacher here. I am not even a scientist in this whole circumstance! Why am I the one that has to figure out everything? Why did I have to be the one to pick up the bread crumbs someone else dropped?"

She stared down at the camera and realized that all of her rant had been captured on the camera because she had inadvertently been filming herself. She took a deep breath and shrugged off her embarrassment. Then a feeling of peace came over her as she began to understand just what roll she did play. She couldn't believe how foggy it had been in her mind and now, just as if someone had brushed away the clouds with one stroke of their hand and brought the meaning into view.

"Okay, here I go." She said to muster up the rest of the courage she would need for her impending task.

She crept slowly with the camera out in front of her as if she were a Green Beret stealthily infiltrating an enemy compound. She made it to the adjoining hallway that connected the corridor with the hall of the studio. She peeked around the corner to make sure no one was there and once she was sure, she resumed her crouched position and continued onward down the passageway and finally reaching Rose's Studio door. As she approached, she could see that there were shadows moving about in the studio but they were indistinguishable. She would have to gain entry into the studio and film the activity up close.

Sally gave the camera the once over to make certain that everything was in perfect working order. She had seen television shows with similar moments and something always went wrong, she was determined not to let those problems plague her quest. The battery had plenty of power, the lens was free of smudges, the light was low but she had one finger on the light button of the camera and when she was well enough into the room, she would press the button illuminating the area and capturing what she saw on the video.

She took a deep breath and reached for the door knob, then the door opened right in front of her and there stood William staring at her as she filmed him.

(IN THE STUDIO)

"Sally, my old friend, you should not be cowering down out here in the hall. You are always welcome in my studio. Come on in!"

Sally was frozen in fright for a moment but once she saw how welcoming William was, her fear was laid to rest and that allowed her to regain her thoughts about the situation. She stood in the open door for a moment as she quickly rewound the footage and watched it back. She immediately noted two oddities. The first, was William's welcome to HIS studio? This was not his studio but Rose's, he hardly ever came in there. The next thing she noticed, which was even more bizarre, was that William's eyes had changed color? His light blues had now turned to an emerald green. The way Rose's eyes had looked. Sally put the camera back on record and refocused it on her friend.

"Well, don't just stand there come on in. It has been a while since I got to talk to my best friend and it will be the last time for a while I believe or hope." William said.

Sally kept the camera focused but now noticed another oddity. William's voice had a definite feminine touch to it and in fact it sounded exactly like Rose's voice. Sally slowly moved forward as she filmed, getting closer and closer to her friend. She finally, arrived at the painting to see William sign Rose's name to the work of art. When he had finished, he looked up into the camera.

"There I am done. I am ready for my close up Madam Director." William said as he held out one arm to welcome her and the other to guide her to the painting.

Sally still could not fully grasp everything but continued to film as she sat down on a small box, the only seat available and brought the entire canvas into view. She lost her breath for a moment as she took in the painting, marveling at the picturesque landscape. The scene was one of a beautiful forest with the early morning sunlight making the droplets of dew sparkle on the leaves as two young wolf pups frolic in a grassy little glen. The two wolves bore an undeniable resemblance to Marcus and Anna, right down to the heart shaped 'birthmarks' in their fur.

Sally looked to the area that she knew was not complete. The space was no longer void of images and in that space she had imagined a breathtaking skyscape however she noticed that she could not see the sky there because a natural observatory made of rock now occupied the area and it was not just a hunk of rock but resting the rock observatory, were two adult wolves staring down, watching like proud parents would as their children played below. The painting went to even greater detail than just two wolves, theses two wolves had a striking characteristic of their own too. It was not heart shapes in their fur but the differences were in their eyes. One wolf had pale blue eyes and the other's eyes had a profound green tint that made its eyes seem like glowing emeralds glistening in the light.

"Well, what do you think?" William asked bringing Sally out of her trance.

"About . . . . painting   is . . . . amazing . . . . Rose?"   Sally stuttered and finally managed to ask the question she had wanted to ask but was afraid she would get an answer.

"Of course it is my work silly. I am the artist in this family. Poor William cannot even paint a fence one color."

"How is this possible?! You are dead! How are you . . . ?" Sally asked but was interrupted by Rose's explanation.

"It is possible because all things are possible with The Creator." William/Rose said.

"The Creator of what?"

"Everything."

"This is what Jack meant by 'possession'! I thought it might be something like this but never thought it would be this because this is too weird! This is too impossible! This is just crazy! How are you able to do this?!" Sally asked motioning her hands up and down highlighting the body in front of her, unsure of what to call the person in front of her because the body talking to her belonged to William but the voice, eyes and presence was that of her best friend Rose.

"You are talking to me, your friend Rose. I know this is odd to you but He gave me this opportunity to come back and help all of you and I was not about to waste it. I saw how devastated William got and I knew you and Malcolm would try to help him but you would have failed miserably. So, I came back, a little at a time and just to William."

"Why did you not come to me? I was your friend long before you met William? Why was I left out of the loop?"

"You and I are still the best of friends and we will always be that but what William and I have is greater than friendship and stronger than family. I do not know exactly how it happened but we are soul mates. You see when we were married, we did not just join our flesh but we joined our souls. That is why he is able to see me in my true form and you have to see me as I occupy his flesh."

"Is he . . . . dead?" Sally asked sheepishly.

"No, far from it. I can only take over when he sleeps. Right now he is examining the painting and I told him that you and I were going to have a 'girl talk'."

Sally looked at the painting and then back up at Rose/William. She could not wrap her mind around the situation. She was standing there having a conversation with her best friend who had been deceased for a little while now but she was looking at her friend's husband as they conversed. Sally rubbed her eyes and then ran her hands over her forehead and through her hair as a gallant attempt to regain her composure but when she looked back up, she still saw William standing in front of her. She just put her face in her hands and groaned.

"Sally, don't look at me like a person but instead look at me the way you would look at a lump of clay or a slab of marble. You must look at me with your heart and not your eyes." Rose said as she put her hands on her disturbed friend to comfort her.

Sally listened to what Rose had said and let those words reverberate over and over in her mind like an echo would in a large cascading canyon. She began to picture a block of clay and looked at it to see what she wanted to create and the emotion she wanted to pour into the piece. Then she felt a peaceful feeling wash over her like before but instead of hardening her resolve, it brought her a feeling of love and devotion that exists between compassionate siblings. The Philia kind of love that ardently binds people together in a powerful friendship that can resemble a familial bond.

Sally looked up with renewed focus and stared directly into her friends deep green eyes. She noticed that William was no longer standing before her but her friend Rose stood there smiling down at her. Sally was speechless as she stared in amazement at her friend. The last time she had seen her was at the funeral and she had looked so frail and pitiful, a lifeless shell occupying a coffin that seemed to dwarf her embattled body. Now, the friend she saw before her was back to herself again with no trace of cancer or chemotherapy that had plagued her body, she was whole again. The white dress that she always worked in was free of tears or stains and shined with all of the radiant glow in a Sunrise.

"Rose, you look beautiful!" Sally said with tears in her eyes and overwhelming emotion in her voice.

"Thank you, Sally. I feel beautiful for the first time in a long while."

"How did you transform like that?" Sally asked as she quickly looked Rose up and down.

"I didn't transform, you did, in a matter of speaking. You are now looking at me with your heart and the heart sees the world as it is, in its true form not like the eyes tell us. Human Beings learned ages ago how to trick the eye into seeing what they wanted it to see but the pure heart sees the truth."

"What happens now?"

"Now, I must go."

"Where?" Sally asked

"Hopefully, where you and all of my family will go someday . . . . Home." Rose answered.

"Do you have to?"

"Yes, but not because I have to it is because I want to. Don't try to understand this aspect because you just have to experience it. What I need you to do is explain everything I have just told you and this painting. William will be able to help you but in the end it will be you explaining what happened here."

"Who will I be explaining it to?"

"Malcolm and William and probably Jack and his associate. It will be William's job to tell everyone and anyone who will listen but that will come later. You just need to fill in the gaps to him."

"How will I do that?"

"Don't be concerned with the words, just trust your heart like you are doing now and the words will come to you. Now, I need you to take your camera and recover your strength because you have been up a while and tomorrow will prove to be a busy and trying day for you and William."

Sally left the room giving her sister one last hug and took the camera with her. She replayed the footage that she had recorded. As she watched she still had a hard time accepting it but knew it had happened. She began to wonder how to tell Malcolm about the event but for now she just wanted to get some sleep.

Rose returned to William's side as he stared in awe, at the painting. It was in fact her Magnum Opus but more to the point it was their 'family' portrait. William scratched his head as he looked at the painting and noticed that Rose had returned from her talk with Sally.

"What troubles you my loving husband?" Rose asked staring at him with her warm eyes.

"I can accept a lot, I have accepted a lot but one thing I must know is how did you know about the kids and the anomalies with their fur and even the color patterns of their fur? I never got the chance to show them to you and I never brought my work with them home because they were still very young when you got sick. How did you guess right about all of this?" William asked.

"William, you have been through quite a bit I will admit but it is your heart that has brought you through it all and not your wits. Your wits would have led you to a mental asylum and I would have never finished this work of art . . . . of our family."

"What exactly does that mean?"

"You are an extremely intelligent man. In fact you are the smartest man I have ever known but there are some events in life that require one to put aside his or her vast intellect and trust that their heart will tell them the truth, you did and we finished the painting together. Just as you have used my heart to focus on me, I used the images in your heart to get the pictures I needed for this painting."

William looked back at the canvas and smiled. This whole event had not made any sense until now and he knew that it probably would not make sense to anyone else but he knew what happened because he believed. Belief had gotten him to his understanding.

"They really are beautiful kids." William said.

"Oh, they are magnificent! Your gesture of the revealing of the kids to me would have been extremely sweet and touching and I hope our endeavor here will be cherished by many because it is a product of our love. That after all is what all parents want, for their children to be shining examples of the love their parents shared and to take that love and share it with the rest of the world. I am sorry I could not give you a child of your own but I do hope that you will find someone to have children with someday. Do not let death or depression turn your warm heart cold, for in this world is a heart frosted from hurt suffered by lesser men and she is in dire need of the loving warmth your embrace can provide."

"There will never be another like you, Rose." William said with tears flooding his eyes.

"You will always have a piece of my soul and I a piece of yours. That is the bond that we share. You will love again, in time, because while you and I share pieces of a soul, you still have a heart to share. We will have all eternity to be together later but for now tell others of what happened here and try to get them to embrace faith the way you have here and never know loneliness again. I love you, William."

They embraced and shared a passionate kiss as Rose changed from her physical form to one made of light and in a moment, was gone. William looked at the Sun struggling to get into the room and pulled back the curtain up the shade to let it bathe the room in light. The painting glowed even more during the light of day and his heart did not feel cold or embattled but at peace. He closed his eyes and stood facing the Sun with both hands over his heart in the studio and reveled in the moment until he heard a knock at the door.

"Come in." He struggled to say as he still kept his eyes closed holding his head up toward the ceiling and his hands covering his heart.

"William, I need to show you . . . " Sally said as she looked at the camera's screen but then stopped in mid sentence when she noticed William's stance. She knew what had just transpired in there and wondered if she had interrupted the tender moment. She pulled the camera into her chest as if to keep the question quiet and stand in revered silence. She felt so embarrassed and started to quietly back out of the room but William stopped her.

"It is okay, Sally. You are not interrupting me." William said as he opened his eyes and turned to look in her direction.

"Is she still . . . . ?"

"She will always be here with me. She and I are linked. We are Soul Mates." William said with a great big smile.

Sally smiled back fighting back the tears of joy she felt trying escape her. William came and embraced her like a big brother. They had both been through a lot in the past weeks but even more in the past 48 hours. Now, their thoughts turned to how to explain all of the events that had happened but the moment was brought to a halt by a question.

"What is going on in here?!" Malcolm asked standing in the doorway looking at the two of them with his hair all a mess and his clothes disheveled from a night of deep sleep. He rubbed his head and then his neck as he waited for a response but when one did not immediately come, he offered an explanation of his own.

"I just had another crazy dream about Rose but this time, she just told me to get up and come in here to talk with you guys. So, out of sheer morbid curiosity, I did and I find you two in here hugging and crying. What are you two a couple now?"

"No, nothing of the sort. However, we do have a story to tell and some footage for you to view but the real blessing from the story will come only if you trust what your heart is telling you and not just what your eyes see." Sally said.

(IN THE DEN)

She and William spent the day filling Malcolm in on what had happened last night and how all of the events had come together. The mysterious painting, writing on the wall, the dreams and even what Jack had discovered and was rushing back to tell them. Malcolm listened but was prevented from doing so by his own zeal. Malcolm listened trying to dissect the story and the evidence the way a psychiatrist would but at every turn in the revelation, his theories were proven wrong.

Malcolm paced back and forth in the den in front of the television screen that showed the evidence that proved Sally and William's story. Malcolm would pace for a moment, stop when he had a plausible theory but then look at the screen or look at one of them. Then he would shake his head, mutter something and resume his pace. Finally, he came to the only conclusion that he could, even if it were one he did not want to defer to but had little choice.

"Have you told Jack about this? Maybe he could make more sense of it all."

Sally and William shared a glance and a smirk and then, William handed Malcolm his cell phone to call the number the Policeman had given them. Malcolm ignored their grins and feverishly dialed the number. Malcolm stood as William and Sally listened to the conversation on Malcolm's end of the phone.

"They are okay . . . . out of surgery and into a room of their own . . . . why no visitors . . . . oh family only. Well, can we at least talk to him? Great, just give me the number . . . . (Malcolm hurriedly wrote down the number on a piece of paper as he continued to speak with the officer.) . . . . thank you, officer." Malcolm ended the phone call and dialed Jack's room number in hurry as if the questions he had to ask would vanish from his mind if he did not ask them soon.

"Dr. Jack Watson please this is Dr. Hearth . . . . no, the other one . . . . I know of his situation but he was coming to see my family and me when the accident happened . . . . I promise I will not upset him . . . . (Malcolm put the phone on speaker so that everybody else could hear their conversation. They could hear a discussion in the background and when they heard Jack say 'Dr. Hearth' the conversation ended abruptly and then sounds of, what seemed to be a struggle of sorts for the phone were heard.)

"William?" Jack asked.

"No, it is Malcolm but William and Sally are here. We have you on speaker phone so that all can hear you."

"My colleague is out for the moment because of his meds but he can attest to what I am about to tell you, later. The footage I discovered on the camera . . . . "

"Showed a man's arm and then brought the side profile of William into view. Sorry, to interrupt you Jack." Sally interrupted.

"Yes . . . . the officer must have delivered the camera but how did you know where to look?"

"I found your note with the times and the word 'possession' written on it and I just made the connection."

"Excellent work but the question now remains of how this happened and for what reason?"

"Actually, Jack we already know. We had quite the evening last night." William said.

"Well, you guys did? I just had a weird dream and found you two in the studio." Malcolm added.

"What exactly happened?" Jack asked.

"Get comfortable Jack because the story I am about to tell you is not exactly short but then again any story worth hearing is relatively long.""

Sally told Jack all about their past two evenings from the time that Jack had left and bringing him up to the phone call they were having now. Jack's end of the phone had gone silent as Sally finished her account and she feared that Jack had fallen asleep.

"Jack, are you still . . . "

"Oh, I'm here! Only The Good Lord calling me home, could keep me from hearing this story!"

"I was just making sure." Sally said with chuckle in her voice.

"And you have video proof of this event?"

"Yes, we do but while what you see is compelling, it is nothing compared to what we experienced."

"I can only imagine. What does Malcolm think about these facts and events?"

Sally looked over at Malcolm who turned away from her and looked at the wall as if he did not want to give any credence to their story. She then looked at William who looked back at her and smiled as he shrugged his shoulders. They both knew that Malcolm was always going to have problems with this story, even though he witnessed it with his own two eyes.

"I think he was hoping you could make more sense of it for him." Sally informed.

"Dr. Malcolm Hearth wants me to make sense for him. As I live and breathe." Jack said as he laughed.

"Oh, will you just tell us your thoughts already!" Malcolm shouted at the phone and a laughing Sally and William.

"Easy, doctor. You must remain calm. Seriously, I will need to see the video to be certain but I assure you what you have told me speaks volumes that Science cannot refute, the video will only bolster the case. I want to see this painting too. It sounds so very beautiful. The only thing I can add is that the ordeal would have been rough without your faith and perhaps that is what is causing dear Malcolm's frustration, as we speak. Be gentile with him. He will eventually come around, I think. As for you, William, it appears that you have a mission."

"I suppose I do. Get well soon Jack and when you do, I will have a party to unveil the story and the painting." William said.

"I wouldn't miss it." Jack said and hung up the phone.

"William, are you really going to have a party and tell . . . . other people about these . . . . events?" Malcolm asked.

"Yes, Rose always had a party to unveil and sell her paintings. Why should I change that, especially when the painting in question is her greatest achievement?"

"William, I know some . . . . unbelievable . . . . eventsss . . . . have occurred recently but there is a bigger picture to consider here." Malcolm said as he struggled to get the words out of his mouth.

"What could that be?" William wanted to know.

"Your reputation! You are a scientist at a prestigious organization and your work is important to field of Biology and Zoology but if you go public with this story, even with the data you have now, you could lose your status in the community, your funding and even your job. I know Rose gave you a 'mission' but is it really worth risking your livelihood?" Malcolm asked hoping he could insert some rationale into his brother's mind.

"Yes, it is! I have a way of being convincing and I will use that gift to make people see the truth."

"William, please just listen to me! I know I have been wrong at almost everything lately but I am not wrong about this! A reputation is all a PhD has and you are going to come dangerously close to losing it!" Malcolm shouted.

"I don't care anymore! I spent the last few weeks of Rose's life ignoring the stirrings deep within my soul because I was afraid of showing an emotional connection, which I felt would hurt my reputation! I do not plan to spend another minute denying my true feelings about anything ever again!" William argued back.

"Malcolm is right!" Sally yelled and drew the attention of both men all at once. She had been quiet in their recent debate but now decided to enter the fracas on the most unlikely of sides.

"Sally, you are going to take Malcolm's side on this? You were there! You saw what I saw! You felt what I felt and you even caught it on tape! Now, with all of this evidence, you plan to deny the truth?

How can you do that? How can you betray Rose's legacy like that?"
William asked angrily.

"First of all, I do not plan to betray anyone or anything! I do
agree with Malcolm that you should not voice your opinion on this
matter because of your reputation but I can."

"I don't understand?"

"I am an artist. My reputation is in my work! If the public believes
I am . . . . eccentric, then that can only add to my reputation. I can
say that I . . . had help completing the painting . . . . that I had
dreams and in those dreams, Rose appeared to me and told me what
to do."

"William, she is right! A scientist cannot indulge in flights of
fantasy but all artists constantly keep their heads in the clouds, no
offence Sally." Malcolm said.

"None taken, I stopped listening to your churlish comments a
long time ago." Sally sniped.

"So, let me get this straight. You both agree that I should keep
my mouth shut about what I know to be true because I might lose
my reputation but if I take your advice, I might lose something more
much more precious to me, a part of my soul." William stated.

"William, listen to me please. Let me do this, for Rose. I have to
believe that she would not want you to wager your career on this."

William was silent for a time as he contemplated all that had
been discussed. He felt sick to his stomach but he agreed with them.
He prayed that Rose would forgive him but would understand if she
didn't.

"Okay, I suppose you are right. So, what preparations need to be
made?" William asked in a defeated tone.

"Let me take care of everything. This way it will appear that
everything that happened, happened to me and that I am the one
people can choose to believe or not." Sally assured.

"What about Jack and everything we told him?"

"I am sure he will agree with us about this. After all, we are not
denying anything that happened nor are we changing the message

Rose wanted to relate. All we are doing is changing the method that she chose. Instead of you it will be me." Sally assured.

"Except, it is a lie." William sniped.

Sally and Malcolm started to speak to assure William but he threw up his hands in a surrender motion and walked away from them as he spoke.

"It's fine! I am fine! Just do whatever you want."

(TWO WEEKS LATER
AT THE UNVEILING PARTY)

William stood at the podium, on the stage, in the main room of a local community center where Rose and other local artists had always debuted their work. He looked out at the crowd that had gathered all dressed in their finest suits and dresses. It was a who's who of the Scientific and Artistic communities. William and Rose were well noted in the area for the oddity of their relationship because of their chosen professions. However, their communities had respected them for their differences because it added to their charm. Also, they all had witnessed the trials and tribulations that they had recently endured and were eager to see something positive come out of so much suffering.

William moved the cloak back that was concealing the painting, to get a peak at the work of art that they were all there to see. He had made his peace with the plan that they had come up with but he still felt a bit uneasy about the whole situation. He started to feel all of his apprehension about lying come back as he peeked but before he became too engrossed, he was brought out of his trance by a friendly voice.

"Hey, you are not supposed to look at that until we all are allowed to gaze upon it. No cheating."

William spun around to address who had startled him and he saw a familiar face standing before him leaning on a crutch.

"Jack, it is good to see you up and about again." William said.

"It is good to be up and about again." Jack answered.

Jack could see the upset look on William's face. He knew of the plan and could tell that William was less than enthusiastic about it. Jack had agreed to the plan only at William's behest.

"Are you okay, William?" Jack asked.

"I am fine."

"I am . . . . not convinced. I can tell that this 'plan' does not sit well with you." Jack asserted as he put his hand on William's shoulder.

"I just feel like I am letting Rose down. It is as if I just pushed her feelings aside, again."

Jack looked at William as if he were studying his situation, then after a brief hiatus in the conversation, Jack began again.

"When people come to a fork in the road, they weigh the consequences of both paths before accepting one over the other. It has happened all throughout history, Lee taking up arms against The Union, Washington taking up arms against The Crown, and a certain rabbi who chose to death over life."

"I know where you are going with this. I am not a moron." William said wryly.

"I did not say you were but I do not think you actually see my point. I know that you chose this path because you and your family and friends were concerned about your reputation but all of those men were concerned about their reputation as well as their lives but they did not waver with their choice because they believed what they were doing was the right course of action. And you know something, they were right! Now, I know your choice here does not carry the weight of those men, especially the rabbi but sometimes in life we find ourselves worried about what others will think of us and we forget what we think about ourselves. What I am trying to say is, at the end of the day, the greatest critic of the choices you make for yourself will be you. The question you have to ask is, 'Can I live with myself if I do not obey what my heart is telling me?'"

William looked down at the ground and then peeked at the painting again. He stared at the work of art intently and found himself fighting back tears. He felt the strong hand of his friend Jack grasp his shoulder to comfort him again. William reached back without looking and grasped the hand of his friend to let him know that he appreciated his support. William then wiped his eyes and faced his new friend.

"I will support the decision that you make, as long as you make the right one." Jack said jokingly and they shared a laugh so that William could regain his composure.

"Thank you, Jack. I can never repay the all that you have done for me....and my family."

"All that I ask for is your friendship. Also, I still have the original copy of the footage Sally took on my camera. I brought it here to take pictures of this event so if you need the 'raw' footage for an impromptu 'show and tell', just let me know." Jack said as he gave William a wink to let him know he would support a 'daring' plan.

William and Jack shook hands and parted company. Jack staggered off stage, wobbled over to the finger sandwiches and made himself a plate while William remained on stage. William took a deep breath and then went up to the podium. He cleared his throat and tapped the microphone to make sure it was in good working order.

Sally and Malcolm looked on stage to see William at the podium and shared a look of fright with each other. However they were at the back of the room and had no chance of knifing through the crowd to stop whatever William had planned. He was not supposed to speak, in fact they actually did not want him to be there but thought that more questions would arise if he were absent. According to their original plan, he was to be there and stay in the back so that his reputation could be safe.

Sally had prepared all of the invitations taking great care to explain all of the anomalies from her viewpoint and how she had completed the painting for her dear friend. The evening was to be the highlight of the social scene as Sally revealed the painting and took a few questions about the process she used and what she had experienced. All of this was going according to plan until they saw William at the podium.

"Friends, I am glad to see you all here tonight for this special occasion." William announced drawing everyone's attention to his speech.

William's cell phone immediately began to ring and he ducked away to answer it.

"Hello." He whispered angrily into the phone.

"WILLIAM, what are you doing?" Sally scolded.

"I appreciate all that you have done for me Sally but I still have to live with myself. Bye now." William said as he closed his phone.

"This event has brought us all together to . . . " William was interrupted yet again by his phone and he tried to ignore it. " . . . honor my late wife Rose's Magnum Opus." The phone continued to ring and he finally had to address it. "Excuse me."

"HELLO, DANG IT!" He whispered angrily into the phone.

"WILLIAM, you are going to ruin your life!" Malcolm warned.

"It is mine to ruin! Bye." William said and closed his phone.

"What I am about to tell you may shock you but you need to hear the truth. I discovered this work of art just after Rose's death. At her wake to be exact and I wanted to . . . . " William was interrupted yet again by his phone this time he took it out, threw it off the stage and watched as it narrowly missed the trashcan and crashed to the floor. Moans and chuckles were heard murmuring among the guests as William cleared his throat and continued.

William regained his composure and looked out at the crowd to see Malcolm giving him a 'slit throat' sign to tell him to stop. William ignored his brother and looked in a different direction to find Sally holding up her clasped hands in a pleading motion for him to stop but he looked away from her and down at the podium. He knew that their intentions were good but he knew what he had to do. He just wondered if he could summon up the courage, one more time. He took a deep breath and looked back up to the crowd.

"The reason you came here was to honor . . . . Rose." William's voice trailed off as looked at the crowd and saw Rose moving about through the people making her way toward him. William tried to follow her as she weaved through the masses and finally came to an opening where she was in full view. He smiled at her and she to him. His chest swelled with courage and he began with renewed vigor.

"I have a video in my possession that will give you more questions than answers but I will fill in the gaps because this story needs to be told as it happened and from the person it happened to . . . . me."

The End

CPSIA information can be obtained at www.ICGtesting.com
Printed in the USA
235653LV00001B/38/P

9 781456 868963